# Claimed by the Orc Prince

Lionel Hart

Copyright © 2021 by Lionel Hart

Illustrations by Houda Belgharbi: http://www.houdabelgharbi.com/

Cover design by The Illustrated Page Book Design: https://theillustratedpage.net/design/

All rights reserved.

No portion of this book may be reproduced in any form without written permission from the publisher or author, except as permitted by U.S. copyright law.

# Contents

1. Chapter One — 1
2. Chapter Two — 21
3. Chapter Three — 29
4. Chapter Four — 41
5. Chapter Five — 59
6. Chapter Six — 81
7. Chapter Seven — 95
8. Chapter Eight — 111
9. Chapter Nine — 131
10. Chapter Ten — 143
11. Chapter Eleven — 157
12. Chapter Twelve — 173
13. Chapter Thirteen — 183
14. Chapter Fourteen — 193
15. Chapter Fifteen — 211

About the Author — 226

Also By Lionel Hart — 227

# Chapter One

On the morning of Taegan's wedding day, he arrived at the archery range at sunrise. It was not a joyful or even pleasant morning, and it was only the repetitive exercise keeping his attention that pushed down his frustration. Never in his life had he imagined his wedding day would be like this.

A few hours after sunrise, he was joined by Kelvhan, a warlock in the service of the royal library. They did not speak, but Kelvhan watched quietly as Taegan fired arrow after arrow, most hitting the bullseye of each target, but some not quite hitting the center. As the morning stretched on, they remained silent; everything that needed to be said had already been spoken, and Taegan knew they were only enjoying their last secret moments together. Although, he could hardly say he was enjoying the moment—the tension unspoken between them was far from pleasant.

Around mid-morning, Taegan's attendant approached them from the castle.

"Prince Taegan, the king has requested your presence in the main courtyard," he said, keeping his gaze carefully away from Kelvhan. "The procession is arriving."

Taegan sighed, and pulled the quiver off his hip, ignoring the way his fingers trembled. "I'll be there in just a moment," he replied, his eyes flicking over to Kelvhan's for an instant. "Leave us. I'll catch up."

"Of course," his attendant, Aerik, replied, bowing his head before walking back the way he came. Taegan watched him leave, then turned to face Kelvhan again. The other man's face was grim.

"This is goodbye," Taegan said slowly, stepping toward him. He touched Kelvhan's arm; Kelvhan met his gaze for only a moment before looking away.

"For now," he replied tersely, and Taegan lowered his eyes. Each time they had spoken, he still clung to the hope things would change, lingering in denial about what was happening. But Kelvhan seemed to sense his thoughts, and added, "I know. It is your duty. But I... I will miss this."

"I know," Taegan said. He could think of nothing else to say.

Kelvhan helped him retrieve the rest of his arrows, and took his bow and quiver so he could leave quickly. Their hands touched as he passed over the equipment, and they shared one last look before Taegan turned, and was gone.

He pulled a formal robe over the clothes he was already wearing—no point in changing now, when his servants would bathe and dress him in the early afternoon in preparation for the wedding. It took only a few moments for him to make his way to the main courtyard, where his father and a small cohort of royal guards were waiting.

King Ruven was already dressed in his finery, although it was rare for him not to be dressed exquisitely anytime he might be seen in public. The elven king nodded at him as he approached, his long dark hair falling in front of his face as he did so. Taegan responded with a polite bow of his head, coming to stand at his father's side.

"Were you at the archery range?" the king asked. Taegan nodded, and Ruven sighed before reaching over to touch his shoulder lightly. "I know this is not ideal," he continued, still looking toward the main gate of the castle grounds. "But our responsibilities are a double-edged blade. They come with duties as unpleasant as the privileges they allow us to enjoy."

"I understand," Taegan replied, and truly he did. As the only child of King Ruven and the late King-Consort Alain, his other father, he had known since childhood that it was all but impossible that he might marry for love alone. But he had expected to marry another elven noble, perhaps even a human royal, to strengthen the ties between nations. To marry a sworn enemy of the elves, the enemy he had trained since his youth to fight against and to lead armies to conquer—this was unprecedented in all aspects.

"You are bringing about a new era to our people. Hopefully, an era of peace that will outlive us both," the king continued. Taegan nodded tersely, hoping his frustration was not as apparent on his face as it felt. A small, petulant part of him protested that he did not *want* peace; he wanted to be a war hero, to lead his people to victory, to achieve the destiny he'd always been told was his for the taking and that he had worked toward for as long as he could remember. This did not feel like a victory, even if the peace treaty was certainly a milestone achievement in its own right.

The king squeezed his shoulder briefly, then pulled away from him. They both stood, watching the gate—in the distance, they could hear the sound of cheering and music drawing ever closer.

When the celebratory sounds were nearly upon them, the gate to the castle grounds opened, and one of their soldiers rode in on horseback. The warrior was in full elven regalia, wearing a polished silver helm adorned with two delicate, antler-like protrusions—though any elf would know the horns were far more deadly than they appeared with their ends sharpened to a wicked point. The soldier pulled her horse to a stop, and shouted,

"Presenting the Warlord Hrul Bonebreaker, and the full Bonebreaker clan. Do you welcome these guests, my king?"

"I welcome our guests," Ruven replied steadily, and the soldier rode on toward the castle. Behind him, the orc procession followed, led by the man who must have been Hrul Bonebreaker himself.

Taegan had never seen the warlord in person, but Hrul was the largest orc he had ever witnessed—easily pushing eight feet tall, he was a fearsome sight with massive tusks protruding from his mouth, tattoos covering his body and creeping up his shaved head. Even the horse he rode was the tallest beast Taegan had ever seen, and most of the orcs arriving were on horseback as well. He observed the group closest to Hrul, presumably his wife and many children, one of which he was to wed later that very day. A female orc rode to the right of Hrul, and to the left another male, just as large and brutish looking—likely his eldest son. Taegan did his best to ignore the cold, sinking feeling that coursed through his whole body before settling in his gut.

But before he could get a close look at the rest of the procession, Hrul raised up his massive greataxe—though the weapon looked as tall as Taegan and twice as heavy, he lifted it as easily as Taegan might raise a broom over his head.

"King Ruven," the orc called out—his voice was gruff, but he was speaking clear elvish. "I have come to honor the terms of the peace treaty between our people."

"I welcome you, and your clan," the king replied; though he spoke loudly, he did not shout, and the rest of the din had died down so he was still clearly heard. "Today is a day of celebration, one I hope will be recognized as the beginning of unity between our nations for generations to come."

"We shall feast!" Hrul exclaimed, and a roar of agreement rose from the orc procession. King Ruven nodded in acceptance, and he glanced toward Taegan, who nodded quickly as well.

"We will meet in the great hall," Ruven said, before turning to go. Taegan followed, as did the royal guard. He got one last look at the orcs before proceeding down the castle hallway—Hrul appeared to have many children, but one figure near him seemed smaller than the rest. Taegan did not get a clear view, though, before he turned to follow his father back into the castle.

The great hall was already prepared for their arrival—in fact, servants and workers had been preparing it for the past several days. It was decorated for celebration, although there were fewer tables spaced out much further apart than usual, to accommodate the size difference of their guests. Ivy crept along each window, flowers adorned the walls, and magical globules of light floated near the ceiling to illuminate the room like many tiny moons. The room was peaceful for only a moment until the opposite doors swung open and the procession of the Bonebreaker clan and the accompanying elven warriors entered, followed by an entourage of elven nobles attending the wedding.

It was not the elven custom to feast before a wedding, but the orcish custom, so as an act of good faith, they would first dine then prepare for the ceremony, which would then occur in the early evening. Though the appetizers set out looked splendid, and from the smell of it, he knew the rest of the food would be just as delicious, Taegan had little appetite. He sat next to his father at the highest table and took a small sip from a goblet of honey-wine.

"Warlord Bonebreaker," King Ruven said after everyone had found a place. "I present to you my son, the sole heir of Aefraya, Taegan Glynzeiros." Taegan raised his glass and nodded his head in acknowledgment as a few cheers rose from around the room.

"And to you, King Ruven Glynzeiros," Hrul Bonebreaker replied. "I present my third son, Zorvut the Relentless, to join our families." He gestured to the orc sitting across from him—the smaller figure Taegan had seen. While the orc was still certainly nearly seven feet tall, if not more, he was noticeably shorter than his father and siblings. His features seemed somehow softer, his tusks less pronounced—while the sides of his head were shaved and the remaining jet-black hair pulled back into a short ponytail, he did not have any of the visible tattoos Hrul had. The smaller orc, Zorvut, nodded in acknowledgment as well—like Taegan, his tight-lipped expression was barely passable as a smile.

Rather than the applause that had greeted Taegan, an icy whisper spread through the room. Ruven hesitated, then replied carefully,

"I apologize, you said your third son?"

"Yes, Zorvut is the third of seven, and an accomplished warrior. Do not let his stature fool you. We call him the Relentless, as he has never backed down from a fight," Hrul continued, raising his own glass. His tone was still jovial, as if he had not noticed the sudden change in mood—or he was ignoring it. Now Ruven visibly paused, glancing at Taegan briefly before speaking.

"With all due respect, of course," he started, speaking slowly as if testing each word before it left his lips. "I understand our customs differ, but it is customary for the eldest of two families to be matched, so each heir is on equal footing."

Hrul laughed aloud, causing another chill to spread through the room. "Perhaps this is your custom, King Ruven. It is not ours. I can assure you, of all my children, Zorvut will adapt best to elven life. If you ask for my eldest, Zesh, well, I cannot promise he will be as well-behaved. He's best off with me, where he won't need to worry about his temper. My second is my daughter, and if I understand elves correctly, this son of yours would do just as well with another male. She would make a better peace offering to the other tribes."

Time seemed to slow down as Taegan looked quickly between his father, who had already opened his mouth in protest, and Zorvut. The orc had averted his gaze, but looked visibly pained at the conversation. His smaller stature was less intimidating, his expressive face more relatable and understandable—his appearance did not strike fear into Taegan's stomach the way the warlord had. The decision seemed obvious to him.

"I'm afraid I must insist—" Ruven started, but before he could continue, Taegan stood up quickly, startling him into silence.

"I accept your offer, Warlord Bonebreaker," Taegan said, willing his voice not to tremble or break. He glanced back at his father, who was looking at him with a raised eyebrow but an otherwise unreadable expression. "Please, Father, I have no desire to create any further conflict. If the warlord deems this son his best offering, I trust his judgment and I will gladly accept."

Slowly, King Ruven glanced away from his son and gave a single nod of acceptance.

"Ha!" the warlord exclaimed. "This one has a backbone to him. What an elf!" Taegan looked back over at the table of orcs—Hrul had a pleased, almost smug grin around his tusks, but Zorvut had a look of genuine surprise on his face. Their eyes met, and Taegan gave a terse nod of acknowledgment. After a moment, Zorvut returned the gesture with some hesitance, then looked away, his expression reminiscent of shyness. It may have just been the light, but from a distance, it looked like he might be blushing.

When Taegan sat back down, he realized the music and chatter had resumed around him. The king leaned closer to him and said quietly, "You deserve more than their runt, my son."

"I would rather have him than a fight," Taegan whispered. "And besides, he looks the least likely to rip me in half with his bare hands."

King Ruven gave a single chuckle at that; Taegan knew he was not truly amused at his words, but he hoped his father understood.

"You sacrifice much," Ruven finally sighed, lifting his own goblet of honey-wine to his lips. "I only hope it is not in vain."

When the meal was done, Taegan went to his private quarters to prepare for the ceremony. His hand-servants bathed him in warm rosewater and lavender soap, brushing and smoothing his long, light brown hair before braiding a few sections that were then pinned to his ceremonial crown. His outfit had been laid out for him as well: a silky, high-collared tunic gilded with fanciful swirls embroidered in silver and dotted with jewels, white form-fitting breeches, his finest boots, and a long cape in the traditional silver and navy blue, dotted throughout with small gems like stars on a night sky.

As the cape was being laid over his shoulders and affixed in place, he heard the latch of his door open. Glancing back, he saw Kelvhan enter and close the door softly behind him—though he would normally be glad to see the other man, this time his appearance wracked Taegan with guilt.

"You shouldn't have come," Taegan said stiffly, turning away from Kelvhan to look straight ahead as his attendant pinned the cape in place, carefully averting his eyes from the unexpected visitor.

"You don't need to do this," Kelvhan said, stepping closer to Taegan. "Gods, I saw the brutes entering the castle—how can your father be doing this to you? Truly, Taegan, to *marry* an *orc*—it's absolute foolishness!"

"I don't expect you to understand," Taegan replied, frowning as he glanced back at him. "But it is my duty to our people to ensure this peace treaty remains in place."

"It's not too late. Please. Let's just go," Kelvhan insisted. "We can leave right now. I know a wizard in Autreth, I'm sure he would harbor us until…"

"Until what?!" Taegan snapped, finally succumbing to his anger as he whirled around. Aerik's hands fell away from him and the cape with them. "Do you think I wanted this? Do you think I trained my whole life to lead the fight against the orcs just to be married off to one as soon as I come of age? Kelvhan, please—" At that, his voice broke, and he turned away. He sucked in a heavy breath to steady himself before continuing, "Kelvhan, we could not have been together in the long run regardless of the peace treaty. The time we had together was enjoyable, but it's over now. I'm sorry. This is already difficult for me. Please, just go."

He did not turn around, so for a long moment of silence he did not know how Kelvhan had reacted—but after what felt like an eternity, he finally heard more footsteps, and the door thudding shut again. Taegan breathed a sigh of relief.

"He left?" he asked quietly.

"Yes, my prince," Aerik answered just as softly, glancing back at the door before bending down to grab the cape again. Taegan squeezed his eyes shut and took in a few deep breaths, trying to slow his pounding heart as Aerik re-affixed the cape around his shoulders.

It took a few moments, but when he opened his eyes again, the cape was pinned in place and Aerik was nearly done. With a final tug of the cord that kept it tied and a careful smoothing of the floor-length fabric, Taegan was fully dressed in the ceremonial garb.

Hardly realizing he'd been walking, he soon found himself standing in the courtyard leading into the temple tree where the ceremony was set to take place. His father had changed as well, wearing ceremonial robes similar to his own but more subdued, featuring more navy blue compared to his silver garb. The crown he wore was one of the more elaborate, formal pieces, much larger than the one Taegan had. King Ruven bowed his head in greeting and managed a small smile, though Taegan could tell it was strained.

"My son," he said. He hesitated as if he wanted to say more, but instead simply placed a hand on Taegan's shoulder, squeezing it firmly. Taegan did his best to smile back, though he could feel it waver.

Taegan glanced beyond the willow tree that acted as something of a curtain between the paved courtyard where they stood and the soft dirt and grass of the outdoor temple. He could see a few figures had gathered at the giant tree where the visages of the gods were carved, which served as the centerpiece of their temple; he could make out a handful of elven nobility, and the much larger orcish figures that were waiting for his arrival.

"Ready?" his father asked, noticing him glancing beyond the courtyard. Taegan took in a long, slow breath, then nodded.

Together, they walked into the temple. His father's court bard was playing a soft tune on the harp, and the high priest stood before the giant tree, also dressed in ceremonial robes. The branches of the tree temple partially obscured the late afternoon sun, its dappled light coming through in small patches in the shaded grove. Whatever quiet chatter had been happening trailed off as Taegan and the king approached. Each of the elves lowered their heads in a slight bow upon their arrival, including the priest, who then beckoned them up to where he stood, where Zorvut was waiting as well.

The orc was in ceremonial garb, too—or, at least, what Taegan assumed was ceremonial garb for orcs. He was shirtless but wore a fine bear fur cape around his shoulders that went down to his waist, tight breeches and leather boots. His hair, which had been pulled into a high ponytail when Taegan had first seen him, was now loose with a few braids similar to his own that fell just past his shoulders. But the most striking feature was the war paint adorning his body and his face; a vivid blue that stood out in stark contrast to his grayish-green skin. The paint brought attention to his yellow eyes, making them appear a vibrant golden color, and created a series of symbols from his collarbone to his hips, though Taegan did not know what they meant.

Their formal wear could not be more different, he thought—yet there was something striking about Zorvut's appearance, some sort of fiercely powerful air that Taegan found alluring despite himself.

"To all who have joined us today, we thank you," the priest began, pulling Taegan from his thoughts. "I am Estalar Yeloris, high priest of the elder tree temple. And the two we join today need no introduction, I am sure. But with this ceremony, Prince Taegan Glynzeiros and Zorvut Bonebreaker the Relentless will be joined in marriage, a first for our communities. May their union symbolize continued peace between our nations."

A quiet murmur of agreement spread through the small crowd. Taegan could feel Zorvut glancing over at him, but he kept his gaze trained on Estalar, who somehow still had a bored expression as if this were any routine, average wedding.

"Is there any objection to the ceremony?" the priest asked, and for a brief, terrible moment Taegan had a vision of Kelvhan storming in and ruining everything—luckily, when he snuck a quick glance around the crowd, the other elf was nowhere to be found.

No one responded to Estalar's invitation, so he continued, "Then we gather here beneath our elder tree, before each other and the gods, to join these two. Since time immemorial, elves have stood beneath these trees to bind themselves to each other in marriage. The gods have smiled down upon us, that any elf may marry another as an equal and continue our lineage. In exchange for pledging ourselves to one another, the gods give us what is perhaps our greatest gift—our mental bond, formed through ancient magic, so that we are bound not only in word and in heart, but in mind as well."

Taegan could sense Zorvut shift slightly at that, likely in discomfort or surprise. The marriage bond between elves was not necessarily a secret, but neither was it common knowledge—it was entirely possible Zorvut had never heard of this aspect of elven marriage.

"First," the priest continued in the same monotone voice. "Prince Taegan, if you would give your vows to Zorvut."

Taegan took in a long, steadying breath before glancing over at the orc. It was the first time they had really looked at each other as their eyes met—and as he spoke, he realized it was the first time he had addressed the other man as well.

"Zorvut," he said evenly, willing his face to remain cool and expressionless. "This day, I pledge to improve the lives of every elf and every orc in our nations. I will treat you with the respect and honor you deserve. I will support you in your personal endeavors, and guide you in our royal duties as we learn to join our nations together. My heart will be tender toward you and yours, and I will remain faithful to you, my husband. This, I vow to you before the gods and our people."

Zorvut's face was hard to read, but his expression softened somewhat as Taegan spoke to him. While he knew nothing of his betrothed, Taegan had mulled over his vows for several days leading up to the wedding, and Zorvut seemed to recognize the effort he had put into them.

"Do you find these vows sufficient, Zorvut?" the priest asked, and Zorvut nodded.

"Yes," he said—though his voice was gravelly and deep, it was softer than Taegan had expected, and he realized that this, now, was the first time he had heard the orc speak.

"And Zorvut, if you would give your vows to Prince Taegan."

"Taegan," he started slowly, glancing away briefly before meeting Taegan's gaze again. "I vow to be your protector, defender, and greatest supporter. I vow to learn from you to be a good prince, and a good... husband. I vow to give you no cause for distrust, and I vow that our union will remain strong, both between us and between our nations." He paused, then added quickly to echo Taegan, "This, I vow to you before the gods and our people."

"Do you find these vows sufficient, Taegan?"

"Yes," Taegan replied, as they were certainly more eloquent than he would have expected.

"Then please, join hands so I may bind you," the priest said. Taegan extended his hand, and after a brief hesitation, Zorvut followed suit. His hand was easily twice the size of Taegan's, so although they grasped hands, it was more like Taegan holding his fingers. Estalar reached out both of his hands, placing one on each of their wrists, and whispered in elvish.

Taegan had heard the ceremonial incantation many times before, but the sensation of it was unexpected. He could feel heat emanating from where the priest grasped his wrist up his arm, through his shoulder and his chest, pulsing in his heart and spreading rapidly to the rest of his body. It soon faded, except for a pinpoint of warmth near the back of his head. With a final declaration, Estalar pulled his hands away from them, a small glimmer of magical sparks following, and the pinprick of heat blossomed into a painful burn for one unbearable instant—Taegan squeezed his eyes shut—then quickly settled to a more comfortably warm sensation.

For a moment, it did not feel as though anything had happened, but then he could feel confusion and uncertainty emanating from that spot in the back of his head—not his own, but Zorvut's. He took in a long, steadying breath, focusing on the calmness he was trying to hold on to, and Zorvut met his gaze with surprise as the anxiety from his end of the bond settled to a low simmer. It was a strange sensation, but he was sure it must be much stranger to Zorvut; after all, Taegan had wondered since childhood what it might be like to have someone else in his head, while Zorvut would have had all of perhaps two minutes to consider it before having it thrust upon him. Taegan almost felt pity for him, though he quickly reined himself in, hopefully before Zorvut could sense it. It was going to take some getting used to.

"It is done," Estalar declared. "The gods have looked upon this union and smiled in approval. I present to you now, Princes Taegan and Zorvut. May their marriage guide us into an era of peace."

A smattering of applause spread through the small crowd, though Taegan barely registered it. Hands still joined, they turned to face the crowd, and he looked over at his father. King Ruven had a tight-lipped smile. In contrast, Hrul and the other orcs had wide grins and were shouting and cheering.

"We celebrate!" Hrul declared, and King Ruven nodded.

"We will have drinks in the courtyard," he agreed, and gestured for the couple to lead the way. Taegan stepped down from the small platform in front of the elder tree, and Zorvut followed him. He tightened his grip on the other man's much larger hand as they walked, and after a moment, Zorvut very gently squeezed his hand in response.

# Chapter Two

Taegan managed only a single goblet of honey-wine in the courtyard before the polite conversation expected of him became unbearable. He was sure Zorvut could sense his exhaustion and irritation, and in turn he could feel Zorvut's trepidation as clearly as if it were his own.

"Father," he muttered, when one of the visiting nobles stepped away from King Ruven, but before another had a chance to take his place. "I think we shall retire now."

"It's still early in the evening," the king remarked, but upon meeting Taegan's gaze seemed to note the pained expression on his face. "But it has been a long day, to be sure. Not to worry. I will continue to entertain our guests. Get some rest." Taegan nodded gratefully, then turned to Zorvut.

"I will show you the way to my quarters. Our quarters," he said, correcting himself quickly, and Zorvut nodded in agreement. Though he tried to leave without drawing attention to themselves, as soon as they moved toward the entrance to the castle, a raucous cheer rose up from the orcish side of the party. Taegan knew little orcish, but felt quite certain that the word for *consummate* was somewhere in the din, and the sudden embarrassment radiating from Zorvut despite his stony expression was more than enough to confirm.

"Thank you for your presence here tonight," Taegan said hurriedly as it became apparent their exit was noticed. "This is a historic moment, to be sure. Please, excuse us. My husband and I will see you all again tomorrow, I'm certain." Luckily, he had practiced enough to not trip over the phrase *my husband,* though a slight thrill of surprise and something like excitement rose up from Zorvut when he said it. His emotions were just similar enough that Taegan could name them, but still felt distinctly different from his own, and he wondered how foreign his own feelings might be to Zorvut.

The elves in the crowd all gave him polite smiles and nods, but another shout and cheer rose up from the orcs, and Zorvut replied gruffly in their own tongue. His family members laughed, then waved them away, seeming satisfied with whatever Zorvut had said. Taegan moved toward the castle, and Zorvut followed.

They passed a handful of servants in the halls, who each stopped and bowed politely as they walked by—Taegan barely noticed them, preoccupied with his own thoughts. Though he had escaped the crowd, being alone with his new husband was its own ordeal he would have to face when they arrived in his bedroom. *Their* bedroom.

He paused when they approached the stairs that led up to his bedchamber. The spiral staircase was rather narrow, and he looked back over at Zorvut. It would be a tight squeeze.

"I'll fit," Zorvut offered abruptly, sensing his thoughts.

"There's a different staircase at the other end of the hallway that I can show you tomorrow," Taegan said. Zorvut seemed confused, but did not press any further, instead following Taegan up the stairs with his head carefully lowered.

Aerik was sitting, waiting, at the door to his room, his usual post. Zorvut gave a slight start when he noticed the elf, but Taegan waved him away quickly.

"Leave us," he said. "Do not disturb us until tomorrow morning."

"Of course, my prince," the servant replied, bowing his head gracefully, and brushed past them descend the stairs. Taegan opened the door, and Zorvut ducked to step inside.

His rooms had been tidied, of course, and the servants had moved many of his personal belongings to his own private study in anticipation of their newly shared quarters. It was warm enough now, in the height of springtime, that the fireplace was not in use, but a handful of candles had been lit and placed throughout the room, atop the dressers and each bedside table. The massive bed was new as well, easily triple the size of Taegan's previous bed, taking up a significant portion of the chamber. Even glancing at it made Taegan feel suddenly embarrassed, and he could sense the same emotion coming from Zorvut, too.

The door closed behind them, and Taegan let out a long sigh, steeling himself. Zorvut stood awkwardly in the entryway, obviously uncertain about fully entering the room. He seemed to understand Taegan's trepidation, though, as he offered quietly, "We don't have to—"

"Will you help me take this off?" Taegan interrupted, gesturing at his cape, but still not looking back at Zorvut. It was his duty, he repeated to himself. "It's... difficult to unpin on my own."

Zorvut paused, seemingly taken aback, then stepped closer to Taegan. He placed his hands on the elf's shoulders, feeling along the cape for the pin before carefully removing it. The cape fell around Taegan's feet, and Zorvut gingerly placed the gleaming silver pin in Taegan's hands, which he set onto a bedside table.

Finally turning to face the orc, Taegan started to unbutton his shirt. Their eyes met for only a moment, then Zorvut's gaze fell to Taegan's fingers deftly exposing more of his chest as the shirt loosened. To his surprise, desire zapped through their bond—hesitant, but unmistakable. His hands fumbled, and Zorvut reached out to clasp them.

"Let me," he said, and he finished unbuttoning the shirt. Taegan could feel the heat searing through his face, something like embarrassment or shame—Zorvut paused, looking askance at him, and despite himself Taegan gave a quick nod, and the orc pulled his shirt off entirely. His large, rough hands brushed against him as he did, leaving a trail of warmth where they passed. Cutting through his uncertainty, Taegan could feel the familiar ache of arousal between his legs.

Zorvut could surely sense both of his conflicting feelings, and after a moment of hesitation, he gently pulled Taegan's hands to his own torso. The orc's skin was rougher than his own, but the hard ripple of muscle underneath was unlike anything Taegan had ever felt before, and he ran his hands up from Zorvut's abs to his chest, letting them rest near his collarbone. He could not tell if the pleasure he felt was his own or Zorvut's.

"I did not know about this part," Zorvut said, and when Taegan looked up at his face, he could see the orc's eyes were squeezed shut. "I... I am sorry. I did not want to be untoward. This makes it more difficult than I expected."

"You cannot be untoward to me," Taegan retorted. "I am your husband." The declaration sent another bolt of desire through him, through their bond—what had started as a tentative interest was quickly growing irresistible in the feedback loop between them. Spurned into boldness, Taegan let his hands trail along Zorvut's chest once more, this time drawing lower to his waist. He could feel Zorvut hesitate again, but before he could stop him, Taegan untied his breeches and pulled them down.

Taegan had been with other men, of course, some of them quite a bit bigger than himself. And part of him had known that although Zorvut was smaller than the other orcs in his family, he was still much, much larger than Taegan, and that would certainly apply to every part of him. He knew that, but still he was taken aback at the massive cock freed from Zorvut's tight leather breeches. He could only bring himself to look for a brief moment before glancing away, the surprise quickly morphing to fear as he considered the orc's member seemed easily the size of his own forearm. Instinctively, he pushed against Zorvut's abs, though he did not succeed in moving the orc at all and instead took a quick step away.

Immediately, the desire he had felt through the bond turned cold, and embarrassment flooded through the spot in the back of his head where it had settled. Taegan squeezed his eyes shut in his own shame, and he could hear Zorvut pulling his breeches back up.

"I—" he started, his voice breaking. He cleared his throat. "I apologize."

"No, don't," Zorvut said, his tone equally rough. "I understand. I don't want to do anything you don't want to do."

Though the words were meant to assuage him, they only made Taegan more frustrated.

"We could try something else?" he offered, but his tone was unconvincing even to himself, and Zorvut's gaze remained firmly on the ground.

"Let's not rush anything," he said brusquely, and he reached down to pick up Taegan's shirt, offering it to him. Taegan stared at him for a long moment, but Zorvut did not meet his gaze, so he snatched the shirt and walked away, stepping into the small dressing-room nestled between the main chamber and the bathroom.

Silently, he unbraided the crown from his hair and removed his clothing, though his trembling fingers made it difficult. He could not tell if the hot shame burning through his face was his or the orc's. His sharp, rapid breathing broke the quiet of the dressing-room, and it took him a long moment to slow his breaths enough that his pounding heart settled into a less-frantic rhythm. For a moment, he considered changing into a sleeping robe, but instead stepped back out naked.

But during the time he was in the dressing-room, Zorvut must have gone to the bathroom to wash; he had cleaned off the war paint from his body, pulled a blanket and some pillows from the bed, and was now laying on the floor. Taegan stood in the entryway, willing the orc to look at him now that he was unclothed, to feel desire for him again, but Zorvut was resolutely facing the wall and remained motionless.

"We don't need to rush," Zorvut repeated in a slow mumble, sensing his presence or perhaps his frustration, and Taegan sighed, giving up and blowing out the candles on his side of the room before getting into bed and wrapping himself up one of the many blankets that had been laid out for them. After a moment, he heard Zorvut sit up and extinguish the candles next to him as well.

"Good night," Taegan said into the darkness. He could hear Zorvut shift on the floor—though he could not see, he imagined the orc had finally turned to face him.

"Good night," came the soft reply. Taegan was sure sleep would not come easily, but he squeezed his eyes shut anyway.

# Chapter Three

The next morning, Taegan rose early but found himself alone when he woke. The empty room startled him at first, for he could still sense the presence of Zorvut in the back of his head, making him feel as though he were being watched despite his solitude. He could not pinpoint where Zorvut was from the faint awareness of him in his head, but certainly he was still somewhere in the castle.

He knew that there would be a second celebration in the orc encampment this evening, but until then, his day was largely free. Perhaps, he thought, it would be best if Zorvut did not wander about the castle unattended.

The door opened shortly after he got out of bed, but it was his attendant.

"My prince," Aerik said, his tone as even as ever, as he extended a pitcher of fresh water. "I'll help you dress."

"Were you waiting outside?" Taegan asked, raising an eyebrow. Aerik hesitated, as if considering what to say.

"Your husband asked me to remain nearby when he left for the morning," he finally replied. "He requested that I maintain my usual duties, and help you dress."

Taegan was a bit surprised at that—while he had not expected his personal servants to cease their duties, it was unexpectedly thoughtful for Zorvut to request they continue. He had not considered the change in their routine that his presence might cause.

"Of course," he acknowledged. He proceeded to freshen up and dress for the day, Aerik brushing his hair and fastening his cloak for him. It was a mild spring day, though a slight chill still lingered in the morning air.

Taegan made his way down to the dining hall, leaving Aerik to tidy up his quarters. Halfway there, he passed the library, and paused for a moment. The door was closed, but he was tempted to step inside, just to see if Kelvhan might be on duty—but no, he told himself, to do so would be inappropriate. He kept walking.

"Taegan," a voice called from the corridor behind him. As if his thoughts had summoned him, Taegan turned to see Kelvhan standing halfway between the hall and the corridor, beckoning him over. They were alone, but Taegan still hesitated before joining him in the darkened passageway, one they had used as a secret meeting place many times over.

"You're all right?" Kelvhan asked in a quiet voice. Taegan scowled.

"Of course I'm all right," he replied. "Kelvhan, this is... untoward."

"There is nothing untoward about our relationship," Kelvhan pressed, stepping closer to him. "My only regret is that I did not insist your father call this off before it was too late."

"You have no claim to me," he retorted, struggling to keep his tone even. This was already difficult enough; did Kelvhan really not realize how much harder he was making everything?

"I have more claim to you than some orc you just met," Kelvhan snapped, and grabbed Taegan's wrists. "Listen. I know it's too late to change matters now. But our relationship was already a secret. Why must we end things now? Why can't it just *stay* secret?"

For one wild, fleeting moment, Taegan wanted to agree, wanted to lean into Kelvhan's familiar embrace. It was not the thought of Zorvut that made him pull away, but the thought of the peace treaty his father had fought so hard for falling apart, the thought of all this struggle being in vain, that centered him as he closed his eyes and firmly pulled his wrists out of Kelvhan's grasp.

"I have an obligation to him. I'm sorry," he said softly, unable to meet the other man's gaze. He could hear Kelvhan sigh and take a step back.

"I don't understand," he said, and there was a genuine ring of despair in his voice.

"My duty outweighs my wants," Taegan insisted, then slowly added, "And... Well, I don't know if this is normal. But our bond seems rather... strong, already. I'm sure he could sense if anything happened." He stopped himself from adding that he suspected Zorvut could even sense his own unsettled emotions now.

Kelvhan scowled at that, but looked away in frustrated acceptance. After all, Taegan figured, it would be difficult to argue with ancient bonding magic.

"Fine," he relented, turning his back to Taegan. "If that's truly how you feel... I won't bother you again." With that, he walked further down the corridor—before he could be tempted to follow, Taegan turned around and strode back to the open hallway, hurrying past the library. He did not even turn to look and see if Kelvhan might have followed him until he was halfway to the dining hall, but luckily, when he did finally look, he was alone.

Entering the dining hall, he breathed a sigh of relief, only to feel his chest tighten up again when he saw Zorvut sitting alone at one of the end tables. The dining hall was empty save for him, and he did not look up when Taegan entered. He wore plainclothes now—a loose cream-colored tunic and dark brown breeches, his hair loose and pushed to one side. He made a mental note to have the tailor come and fashion him a more suitable wardrobe.

Steadying himself with a deep breath, Taegan stepped over to his table.

"My husband," he said, and Zorvut's head snapped up, startled. "Your place is at the royal table." Zorvut blinked, then slowly stood.

"Of course," he replied, and Taegan held out his hand. He could feel Zorvut hesitate, and he tried to project calmness through their bond, though he was sure his own trepidation came through more strongly. After a moment, Zorvut gingerly took his hand—his thumb and first two fingers were as much as Taegan could easily grasp—and allowed himself to be led to the head table, which now had three place settings.

"Have you eaten already?" he asked as they sat down.

"Some bread," Zorvut replied. "We are early, so nothing was set out yet."

"Not *that* early," Taegan sighed, and gave two sharp claps of his hands. Almost immediately, a servant came scurrying out from the kitchen.

"My prince," he said, lowering his head in a brief bow.

"Can you bring breakfast out quickly?" Taegan asked, in the firm tone he used to ensure they did not take his question as a request, but an order. "My husband should not be kept waiting." The servant opened his mouth to reply, but seemed to trip over his own words before stammering out,

"Yes, o-of course. I will see to it we start bringing everything out now."

"Thank you," Taegan replied coolly, waving his hand in dismissal. The servant hurried back to the door he came from, pointedly keeping his gaze away from Zorvut. Taegan could feel a faint sense of discomfort radiating from the back of his head. "It will be a learning curve for many elves, I'm sure," he sighed, looking the orc in the face. In the morning light, his eyes were a striking golden shade. "But I promise you, they *will* treat you with the respect due to your station."

"I don't care about that," Zorvut said, his bluntness causing Taegan to blink in surprise—an emotion he had felt irritatingly often this morning, he thought as he glanced away from the orc's unwavering gaze. "Orcs only give respect that is earned. I have always been smaller than the others. But I have always earned respect in the end."

"A noble quality in itself, I suppose," Taegan replied, glancing back up at him. This time, it was Zorvut who looked away. Taegan could not quite place the emotion it elicited from him—but he had the distinct sensation that Zorvut felt he had been misunderstood. Before he could ask, however, the dining hall doors swung open and King Ruven strode inside, followed by a handful of visiting elven nobles as well as his usual attendants and advisors. Some had been mid-conversation, but as they stepped in, they fell silent, seeing Taegan and Zorvut already seated at the head table.

"Good morning," Ruven said primly as he sat down to the left of Taegan, nodding briefly first at Zorvut, then at Taegan. "My son. You're early."

"A bit, yes," Taegan agreed. Zorvut only nodded silently.

"Or perhaps breakfast is late," the king remarked, gesturing at the empty place settings before them. "I suppose that after yesterday's feast, the kitchen may be struggling to catch up."

As if on cue, the servant Taegan had spoken to earlier came hurrying out from the kitchen with a tray of rolls and pastries, followed by a few others each carrying their own trays of food, some with carafes of tea, coffee, and a variety of juices.

"You have coffee," Zorvut remarked in surprise as one servant began to prepare Taegan's usual drink, coffee lightly sweetened with honey and a small amount of cream stirred in. "I had not realized elves commonly drank it."

"Of course," Taegan replied, lifting the warm mug to his lips. "We trade with nations all over the world. Coffee is an expensive import, but quite popular."

"Coffee for you as well, sir?" the servant asked, though his eyes seemed to dart everywhere except Zorvut's face.

"Please," he agreed. "Nothing added." The servant quickly presented the mug to him, and the rest of breakfast was laid out. When three or four more servants had gone by without being able to even look at Zorvut directly, though, Taegan's patience had grown thin. He started to open his mouth to speak as a tray of meats and sausages was unceremoniously placed in front of them without a word, but Zorvut placed a hand over his, stopping him.

"No need," he said quietly, reaching out with his other hand to take the platter, serving himself. "Like you said, they will learn."

It did little to quell his frustration, but Taegan acquiesced, and held his tongue. The rest of breakfast went by at an excruciatingly slow pace, palpable discomfort still radiating between their guests. But King Ruven was as poised and calm as ever, chatting with Taegan and the other nobles as effortlessly as if there were absolutely nothing remarkable about having an orc with him at the head table.

Eventually, Taegan finished his meal, and noticed Zorvut sitting silently with no food left on his plate, either. He leaned closer to the orc.

"We can go," he murmured. "No need to wait for the others." Zorvut simply nodded, but seemed to be waiting to follow Taegan's lead. He stood, bowing his head toward his father, and Zorvut followed suit. Several of the nobles sitting across from them bowed their heads as well.

"Thank you again for your presence during this historic occasion," Taegan said to them. "My husband and I take our leave." Again, none of the elves seemed able to look directly at Zorvut as they bid their farewells. It irritated him, but seemed to elicit no response from Zorvut as they left the dining hall.

"Do you have any plans for the day before the evening celebration?" Taegan asked when they were alone in the walkway. He sensed amusement from Zorvut behind him and glanced back to see him with a faint smirk—perhaps the first time he had seen the orc smile.

"You are more spirited than I would have expected," he said, as if he had not heard Taegan's question. "More... fiery." Taegan raised an eyebrow.

"You expected an emotionless husk?" he asked as he folded his arms across his chest—despite himself, the amusement stemming from Zorvut made him fight back a smile as well.

"That is the stereotype of elves," Zorvut said. "Though I am finding it is more of a front than I would have thought."

"Well, it is the ideal we should aspire to," he replied. "But I am the prince, and if I am a little less austere than someone may like, well, they can complain to my father."

Zorvut chuckled, shaking his head. "I have much to learn about the elves."

For all his bravado, Taegan felt suddenly hesitant, almost shy. "I will teach you, of course," he said before he could overthink the offer. "Now that all the fighting and negotiations are over, I will have more free time. Anything you want to know, I'm sure we could find in the library."

"I don't read elvish," Zorvut said bluntly.

"I'll read to you," Taegan countered. Zorvut did not reply to that, but Taegan could feel something like chagrin in the back of his head. "Now, my original question was if you had any plans for the day?"

"No," Zorvut answered. "I might go to the camp early, to see my family."

"Shall I join you?" Taegan asked, and Zorvut grimaced.

"Perhaps not until the celebration starts," he said, then added, "The new couple being paraded around together is a big deal."

"I will suggest this, then," Taegan said. "You can go to the encampment now, but I'll meet you at the castle gate at sunset, and then we can go together."

"You have plans?"

"I thought I might spend some time in the archery range. Hunting season is almost upon us," he replied. He could feel Zorvut's interest piquing at that, but the orc simply nodded.

"I will meet you at the gate at sundown," he agreed, and started to step away from Taegan, toward the main hall. Taegan grasped his hand quickly to stop him, though he could only grab one of Zorvut's fingers.

"Your clothes," Taegan said. "You'll need finer ones now. I'm going to have my tailor take your measurements. Tomorrow morning?" Zorvut raised a quizzical eyebrow. His face repeatedly proved to be far more expressive than Taegan would have expected of the squat, square features shared by so many of his kin.

"That's fine," he agreed simply, and Taegan released him. The bond tingled faintly as their physical contact ended—he could not remember if he had felt the same strange sensation when he had grasped Zorvut's hand this morning before breakfast. Zorvut seemed to feel the same thing, as he hesitated before turning once more to go.

# Chapter Four

Taegan first summoned the royal tailor to set up a meeting for Zorvut the next morning, then for the remainder of the afternoon he was out in the training yard. His horse had been saddled for him, and for several hours he worked on target practice while riding, as his skills had become rusty since the peace treaty went into effect. The warmest part of the afternoon had passed when he finally dismounted, sweaty and shirtless, to prepare for the evening's celebrations.

He was bathed once more in warm, perfumed water, but rather than his most formal finery he dressed in a simple, fine tunic with a high collar and comfortable breeches, his hair loose and unbraided. He was not entirely sure what to expect of the orcish celebration, but at the very least, it seemed to have a relaxed dress code.

It was shortly before sunset when he left his quarters, only to find his father's attendant waiting for him at the bottom of the stairs.

"My prince, the king requests your presence," the elf said with a politely down-turned gaze—he was one of the oldest elves alive, having served not only Taegan's father but his father before him. "He wishes to have only a brief word with you before your event."

"Of course," Taegan agreed, though it was an unexpected request. But any request of the king could not be refused, so he allowed himself to be led to his father's private study.

King Ruven was dressed in a simple robe and soft fur moccasins, his usual wear when he was out of the public eye—despite the stereotype, Taegan knew his father had little in the way of vanity and preferred to be comfortable whenever possible. His table was a mess, strewn with scrolls and letters as if he were studying, but he smiled at Taegan as he entered.

"Father," he said, bowing his head as the door was closed behind them to give them privacy. Despite Taegan's formality, Ruven stepped forward and put both hands on his son's shoulders with a warm expression.

"My son," he said, observing Taegan's face. He was silent for a long moment, and Taegan raised an eyebrow, uncertain of what he was trying to do. "I trust you are well?"

"Of course," Taegan replied. "Do I seem unwell?"

"You are taking all of this in stride," he remarked, letting his hands fall away from Taegan's shoulders.

He supposed he did seem to be adjusting faster than the other elves, Taegan thought, though even he was not sure how much of that was a brave face and how much was genuine acceptance. For all that he had harangued the servants who could not address Zorvut directly, it was still a struggle to reconcile in his head that the orc was his husband, not an enemy he was strategizing around. His hesitance seemed to betray his thoughts to his father, however, as Ruven's expression softened before he could answer.

"It is an adjustment, to be sure," Taegan said carefully. "But Zorvut is... an interesting character, from what I can tell so far. The warlord was not remiss when he said he might adapt better than any other orc to elvish customs."

"I'm glad to hear it," Ruven said. "I don't mean to be indelicate, but you have found yourselves to be, ah... compatible?"

Taegan flushed, the frustration of last night flooding his mind anew, but found himself nodding quickly despite himself.

"Yes," he lied, desperate to change the subject. "And, well, I wondered if..."

"If?" Ruven prompted, and Taegan hesitated, suddenly unsure if it was a question he truly wanted to know the answer to.

"Father," he said slowly. "How long did it take for you to be able to understand Papa's emotions through your bond?" Ruven smiled at the question.

"It took some getting used to," he answered, a soft expression coming over his face. Though losing Taegan's other father had been painful for both of them, enough time had passed now that his eyes were filled with a familiar look of fondness, rather than despair, when they discussed him. "Even when we both knew what to expect, I would say it took a few months before I could easily distinguish between my emotions and his. So don't fret if it takes longer than that for you, my son."

Taegan remained silent, unsure of how to respond. Already, he had a fairly accurate sense of what feelings were his and what were stemming from the bond. Were they that different, that the presence of Zorvut's emotions was immediately recognizable as alien to his own mind? Or were they instead somehow so compatible that they intuitively knew how to communicate to the other through the bond? He had no idea how they might even tell the difference.

"Some are never able to get across more than basic emotions through their bond," the king continued, seeming to take Taegan's silence as worry. "And, to be frank, we have no actual knowledge of how the mind of an orc might link to the mind of an elf. Unions between elves and humans can vary, so don't concern yourself over it if the connection doesn't come. For some, it always remains simple, and there is no shame in that. It is no one's business but your own—the strength of the bond has no bearing on the legitimacy of your union."

Taegan nodded, but his father's words addressed the exact opposite of his concern. He couldn't bring himself to correct him, though, and simply replied, "Thank you. I will keep that in mind."

"Now," Ruven continued. "I asked you here mainly to tell you to be cautious at the celebration tonight. I understand it is an act of goodwill, and will help solidify the connection between our families for the two of you to be seen together, but there may still be some there who mean to do us—*you*—harm. There will be guards stationed all along the wall, but promise me you won't wander off by yourself."

"I promise," Taegan agreed—though he was sure he could handle himself, staying with Zorvut still seemed like the most logical and safe course of action. Emboldened by the thought, he added, "I have no doubt that my husband will keep me safe."

"Your husband," Ruven repeated, and sighed, glancing away from Taegan. Though he had a diplomat's skill in masking his own emotions, Taegan recognized the fatherly tone in his voice—but whether it was regret or concern or worry or despair, he did not know. Ruven seemed to realize this, though, and quickly masked his expression. "Forgive me, my son. I know all this was my idea, but it is still... an adjustment. I'm sure all parents have a vision in their head of what their children's lives will be like, and I'm sure very few of those ever turn out accurately. But it is still something to reconcile with."

"I understand," Taegan replied, though he could only really guess as to what his father was truly feeling. Although the terms of the treaty originally may have been his idea, Taegan knew his father had been as stunned as he was when the Bonebreaker clan accepted their offer. Part of him wondered if the king would have made the same offer had he honestly thought they would accept.

Ruven did not reply, but instead gave him a gentle pat on his shoulder before turning back to his work.

"That is all," he said, looking away from Taegan. "I'll see you both at breakfast tomorrow, before we see off the procession."

"Of course. Good night," Taegan replied, and as if on cue the door opened back up and his father's attendant let him out.

The strange conversation replayed in his head as he made his way out of the castle, through the grounds, and out to the front gate. The gate was open, and two guards stood watch beside it. They saluted as he passed, making no move to question him. The sun hung low on the horizon, painting the sky a deep gradient of orange, pink, and purple. Taegan paused at a fountain just outside the gate and sat down along its edge—he did not see Zorvut, but here was as good a meeting place as any.

The sense of him was faint in the back of his head, but he could feel Zorvut approaching. He closed his eyes, and if he concentrated, he could feel that sense of him getting closer and closer. When he finally opened his eyes again, he could see Zorvut's form approaching from the cobblestone road. He stood and met him halfway; Zorvut waited for him to approach, then turned to lead him to the encampment.

"The celebration will be... rowdy, compared to the feast yesterday," Zorvut warned him as they started to head through the city. "You should stay close to me."

"I intend to," Taegan replied, peering up at his face as they walked. The further apart they were, the harder it was to feel his emotions, but now that they were next to each other, there was a tinge of sadness leaching from him that Taegan had not expected. He hesitated, unsure if he should say anything. "How was your afternoon?"

"Pleasant," Zorvut said. After a moment, he seemed to recognize the bluntness of his answer, then added, "I said some goodbyes to some friends. The encampment leaves in the morning, and I doubted there would be time between the celebrations and then to do so."

Privately, Taegan wondered if Zorvut had his own Kelvhan somewhere in the camp that he had had to send away. Part of him was curious, but part of him did not want to know—it was not quite jealousy, but something like it. They had each put away their old lives to fulfill the duties set upon them, so perhaps it would be better to let the past lie, especially when it was still in such close proximity.

They made their way down the main road into the surrounding city. While most elves they passed went about their business without much acknowledgment, a few stared openly at Zorvut. A handful waved at Taegan, recognizing the prince, but none called out to him the way they sometimes would whenever he was out on an excursion. The lay folk that lived in the city outside the castle walls often proved to be more amicable and friendly than the endless cycle of visiting nobles within—something about being even this small distance from the tradition of austerity and reservedness made for a very different experience of elfhood. He politely returned the few waves of greeting and recognition he received until they reached the city's open gates, where the sounds of music and celebration could already be heard.

The orc procession had set up their encampment along the wall of the city, spreading alongside it rather than away from it, so tents and bonfires stretched far from side to side as they exited the gate. It was surprisingly colorful; Taegan had expected to see tents in neutral browns and perhaps greens, to blend in with the orc's mountainous home terrain, but every piece of cloth he saw was instead some vibrant shade of red, green, blue, or purple, with no neutral tones to be seen anywhere. Groups of orcs had gathered around small campfires—though it was still quite warm out, the fires seemed to be central gathering-places rather than sources of actual heat. Some were cooking, some were drinking, some playing music or dancing—but as they passed each group, a roar of cheers would rise, many of the orcs raising their tankards or giving a hearty wave to Zorvut as he passed.

Taegan wondered how much he really knew about Zorvut—he was unlike any orc Taegan had heard of, so he had worried perhaps Zorvut was an outcast being offloaded for convenience. But the friendly reception they received, despite some less-warm looks directed toward him, made it seem that Zorvut was overall well-liked. He had had his initial thoughts about who Zorvut must have been, but it was seeming more and more apparent that he did not truly know anything about him at all.

Zorvut must have sensed his conflicted feelings, as he turned his head to glance behind at Taegan even as they walked. "Stay close," he repeated simply, though his eyes lingered on Taegan for a moment before he turned his head back.

After they had passed a long row of tents, their destination became apparent. Several makeshift benches and tables had been arranged in a small clearing, shaded by large awnings of fabrics in a range of colors and patterns, stitched together and strung up on poles. Taegan recognized Hrul Bonebreaker sitting at what seemed to be the largest table with a barrel of ale set up next to him. Zorvut's family members were scattered about the area, but a cheer rose up from many of them as they approached. A jaunty tune began to play, and Taegan could just spot a troupe of musicians set up behind the awning—surprisingly, while one was clearly a half-orc, the two accompanying him were humans. Traveling performers must make do wherever they go, he supposed.

Zorvut led him to a table near Hrul's bench, presumably where he had already been sitting. Some food and drink were strewn messily across the long mead hall-style tables, and he could smell spices and smoke from a little way away, where he assumed more food was being prepared.

"We'll stay here for most of the evening," Zorvut said as he sat down next to him. "But there will be a lot of people coming and going. Some will bring gifts and some will just come to show respect. To be honest, most will probably be addressing my father rather than us."

"I understand," Taegan said, and Zorvut handed him a goblet; Taegan gave it a hesitant sniff when he took it. It was not wine, but had a slightly fruity effervescence.

"It's cider—the closest thing to wine I could get my hands on," he said, noticing Taegan's uncertainty. Taegan raised the goblet to his lips and took a long drink. It was not his first choice, but it would do.

As Zorvut predicted, little interaction seemed to be expected of them. There was a steady stream of orcs coming and going, far more than Taegan would have expected, but the majority seemed to go straight for Hrul, only a handful addressing Zorvut directly and even fewer addressing Taegan at all. Some presented gifts to them—a fresh blackberry pie was the highlight, but most were small trinkets, carved wooden figures or bone amulets, a few weapons, knit scarves, and cloth wall-hangings. The more elaborate gifts all seemed to end up on Hrul's table. Taegan did not quite understand why Zorvut's father received so many of the gifts, rather than Zorvut himself as the one whose wedding was being celebrated, but mostly he was glad that little seemed to be expected of him other than to simply be there.

By the time the sun had fully set and torches were lit all along the wall, it was apparent a small area had been set up for dancing. At first, only a handful of orcs seemed to dance at any given time, but as the night progressed, more and more arrived and danced along to the music that had become decidedly more upbeat and rapid.

"Do you dance?" he asked Zorvut after he had watched for a little while. The orcish way of dancing seemed to involve quite a lot of stomping, clapping, and jumping, a stark contrast to the measured movements and elaborate ceremony of the elven dances he knew. He could feel Zorvut tense at the question, though his expression remained neutral.

"A bit," he replied. "Although it's not my first choice of activity."

"I won't ask you to dance," Taegan assured him. "I only ask out of curiosity."

"Well, they will expect us to join at least one dance before the night is over," Zorvut confessed, glancing over at him. Taegan blinked—while he *could* dance, he was not sure if he could stomp and jump about in a way that might remotely resemble the dancing going on at the moment.

"That's a shame," he sighed. "Do you want to get it over with now?" Zorvut chuckled, much to Taegan's surprise.

"It is you who keeps surprising me," he said, a faint grin forming around the slight protrusion of his tusks. "Alright, then. Let's get it over with." He stood and held out his hand to Taegan. His face felt flushed, though he was not sure why Zorvut's response made him feel embarrassed. Pushing the feeling down, he took Zorvut's hand and allowed himself to be led to the clearing. As they walked, the crowd parted around them—many of the orcs they passed fell silent, watching them closely, but from Hrul's table a loud shout broke through the quiet.

"They dance!" the warlord declared, raising his tankard high, overflowing with ale that spilled onto his arm and the table. "Bards! Give us something merrier, for my son and his elf."

The music paused briefly as the three musicians seemed to consult with each other, then they broke into a loud and rapid beat that elicited a cheer from the surrounding orcs.

Taegan clapped along to the rhythm and gave a little hop, trying to emulate the way the orcs around him were dancing. Across from him, Zorvut began to dance, his movements similar but more fluid, more familiar. As he circled around Taegan, he murmured,

"Just keep doing that." Taegan nodded gratefully, his meager imitation unnoticeable as Zorvut danced along with the crowd.

The song seemed to go on forever, since Taegan only really had two moves to alternate between, but he kept his eyes on Zorvut dancing and leaping around him, and eventually the song came to its end and another cheer rose up from around them. Several of the orcs who had remained to dance slapped Zorvut's back and shoulders, and a few even gave cautious pats to Taegan's back. When they returned to their table, Taegan was surprised to find he was smiling. Zorvut glanced at him, noticing the expression, and managed a hesitant smile in return.

"I must confess," Taegan said to him, leaning close to be heard over the music that had started up again. "I was not sure what to expect of an orcish celebration, but this was not it."

Another tinge of sadness seemed to wash over Zorvut at that, but his expression didn't falter. "Thank you for joining," he said, and gestured around. "It is... comforting, in a way, to have you experience all this before I have to leave it all behind."

Taegan opened his mouth to protest, but could not find adequate words. He supposed Zorvut was right—after all, he was the one leaving behind his people and his culture, the one who would have to adapt to a new home. "Well," he started, considering what it was he wanted to actually say. "It is true elvish customs are much less exuberant, even for celebrations, as you saw. But if the connection between our nations is to remain strong, I'm sure we will make many visits to your homeland as well."

Zorvut waved a hand at that. "There will not be much to miss," he said, making Taegan feel even more confused. He could not seem to get a hold on what Zorvut was really thinking about all this—but the orc seemed to sense his confusion, and grimaced as he looked down at Taegan. "This is the fun part. There are many less fun parts. Most of it, I will not miss. But it is... bittersweet, still, to leave it behind." He hesitated, then added, "It is my home, but you can probably tell I never really fit in."

Taegan nodded slowly, mulling over Zorvut's words. Perhaps his initial impressions had not been so far off after all.

They remained for a few more hours, accepting gifts and well-wishes as they came, but mostly drinking and eating as plate after plate was brought out to them. The dancing and music continued, and by the time Taegan guessed it was around midnight, still seemed to show no signs of slowing down.

"We can take our leave now," Zorvut said to him, and he nodded gratefully.

Zorvut stood and led him by the hand again, but they approached Hrul's table—the piles of gifts had been cleared away, and only his barrel of ale and scattered plates of food remained.

"Father," he said, visibly straightening as the warlord looked toward him. "We take our leave. Thank you for hosting our celebration."

"Go, then, to your new life," the warlord replied—while it sounded dismissive to Taegan, he could feel a faint bead of pride welling up from Zorvut. Then, he raised his tankard and gave a shout, "Tonight we see off my son, and welcome a new era! For Zorvut, the Relentless!"

"The Relentless!" a deafening cheer answered him, as it seemed every orc within earshot responded to his declaration. Zorvut simply nodded his head and turned to go, leading Taegan with him. The cheering and chanting followed them as they made their way toward the city gate. Despite himself, Taegan could not suppress the slight smile on his face as he allowed himself to be led by the hand back the way they came. As they entered through the gate of the city, the guards standing watch nodded at them—with their helmets drawn, he could not see where their gaze was trained, but he liked to think they looked at each of them in turn.

A sudden scuffle behind them pulled Taegan from his thoughts quickly—though not quickly enough, it seemed, as Zorvut yanked him forward as the sound of drawn steel rang through the air, stepping in front of him protectively. Taegan whirled around to see an unfamiliar orc charging them from the gate. He tensed, reaching for the dagger he always kept hidden at his hip, felt Zorvut crouch in a defensive stance—but the two guards were upon him instantly, tackling him to the ground easily despite his size.

"We will never bow to you!" the orc snarled as he thrashed on the cobblestone path, unable to fight off the two elves pinning him down. "Filthy elves! Never! And you, race-traitor! I'll have all your blood, the lot of you!"

One guard raised his sword and brought the pommel of it down hard on the orc's skull. The resounding crack echoed through the street, but the orc instantly fell silent and limp.

"He's drunk," the other said, raising a hand as Taegan started to approach. "No need, my prince. We'll toss him back to the encampment and they can deal with him."

"See to it, then," Taegan said, and turned to go.

"Send him directly to the warlord," Zorvut added, and the coldness in his voice startled him. "Let him know this one disrespects his judgment."

The two guards looked at each other, their faces inscrutable beneath their helmets, then one nodded.

"We will," he answered. Seemingly satisfied, Zorvut turned back to Taegan and followed him once more.

Taegan's heart still pounded in his chest as they walked back to the castle, but he could sense no such adrenaline coming from Zorvut. Maybe, he reflected, he still did not understand the orc as well as he thought he might.

# Chapter Five

Much to Taegan's chagrin, Zorvut still slept on the floor that night, but this time he did not try to talk the orc out of it. In the morning, he was alone again in his room, and met Zorvut in the dining hall for breakfast.

Most of the visiting elven nobles had taken their leave the previous evening, and the orc procession was leaving the city today. They would see them off from the courtyard in the afternoon—Taegan hoped he'd be able to get a decent shirt fitted for Zorvut before then, although he couldn't expect much more than that.

After breakfast, he brought Zorvut to his tailor—the elder elf seemed completely unfazed by him, though Taegan felt quite sure this was probably the first time he had been up close and personal with an orc. He watched as Zorvut removed his plain shirt and the tailor, Elgan, began to drape a soft cloth over him to create a pattern, pinning and marking it with deft, expert hands. After a moment of watching the orc's muscles ripple through the thin fabric, he could feel a tinge of embarrassment leaching through the bond at the same moment Elgan began to wave him away.

"Please, my prince, no need to keep watch," he said, though his eyes remained trained on Zorvut. "I'll be sure he's sent to you in the courtyard at the appointed time."

"Thank you, Elgan," Taegan said, and he turned to go. From the corner of his eye, he could just catch Zorvut watching him leave, but said nothing.

He had a few hours before they would be needed, so he caught up on some of his reading in the meantime. Occasionally he would feel faint flashes of Zorvut's emotions through the bond, though it was not as strong when they were apart. A glimmer of surprise and appreciation, at around the time he had put away his book and started to dress, gave him the hope that maybe Elgan was able to whip up a decent shirt for him after all.

His suspicion was proven true when he arrived at the main courtyard, where both his father and Zorvut were already sitting. King Ruven was dressed in a fine, deep purple silk robe over an embroidered silvery tunic. Zorvut wore a new shirt—Taegan had expected something simple and plain in the short time frame Elgan had had to work with, but the shirt was a deep burgundy with a faint shimmer that complemented Zorvut's skin tone surprisingly well, a slight looseness in the sleeve that became tighter at the wrist and a plunging neckline loosely laced to help display his impressive musculature.

It was much more elegant that Taegan would have expected, a delicate balance between elven fashion and orcish practicality. His appreciation must have been quickly recognizable for Zorvut, who only met his gaze briefly, but Taegan could feel a now familiar, faint tingle of attraction coming from their bond in return.

He took a seat between Zorvut and his father. "It seems I'm late," he said, but the king waved his hand dismissively.

"Nonsense," he replied. "I was here early to enjoy the sun, and Zorvut only arrived a moment ago. I understand he's spent most of the morning with Elgan."

"Yes, I thought it might be nice for him to have a few more princely options to choose from," Taegan said, glancing over to Zorvut, who only nodded in reply. He could tell Zorvut still felt decidedly nervous in the presence of the king, which he supposed was understandable.

Before long, the sounds of the procession could be heard even from the gate. Soon it was flung open, and an elven knight came in on a horse to announce them, much like when the procession had arrived. They were welcomed in, and Hrul and his clan all rode in on their massive horses—despite all the carousing the night before, Hrul showed no signs of a hangover. Briefly, Taegan wondered if orcs even experienced hangovers.

"King Ruven," he called as he came up to the courtyard. "My clan and I thank you for your hospitality."

"We have been honored to receive you as guests," Ruven replied, bowing his head graciously. "And I must thank you once more for your role in this peace treaty. I look forward to the continued good relations between our people."

Hrul nodded, but when he spoke again, he looked to Zorvut. "I bid farewell to you, my son," he said, gesturing to Zorvut. "There is much you carry on your shoulders, but I know you will not be crushed by the weight."

"Thank you, Father," Zorvut replied simply—Taegan was surprised to sense some sadness coming from him. He would have expected Zorvut to feel largely neutral about the whole thing, having admitted he was indeed the black sheep of the family just the night before. Yet he still felt sad to see them go.

"My clan," Hrul called, turning away from the courtyard and raising one fist in the air. "We ride!"

And with that, the procession began their exit. Only a handful of orcs had come to the courtyard, no more than thirty, and each made a short circuit along the stone path to pay their respects to the king and the princes before following Hrul's route back out the gate.

The castle gates closed behind the last rider, Zorvut's gaze lingering on the path for a moment before he turned to look at Taegan. Before either could speak, though, Ruven stood.

"Thank you both for joining me," he said, giving a slight bow of his head. "Zorvut. I understand this will be an adjustment for you, and I want to acknowledge that this arrangement has largely been a sacrifice on your end. Please rest assured that I will do all I can to ensure you're treated well here, and we... I am happy to have you."

It took Taegan a long moment to process exactly what was happening, as this was almost certainly the first time Ruven had spoken directly to Zorvut and Zorvut alone—the same surprise was clear on Zorvut's face. Before he could reply, though, the king looked over at Taegan and gave a small, wry smile.

"My son," he said simply in acknowledgment. "I'll be busy the rest of the afternoon, but I'll see you both at dinner."

"Of course," Taegan replied automatically, unsure of what else to say.

"Thank you, sir," Zorvut added stiffly, something like embarrassment radiating from their bond, though Taegan couldn't quite place it.

Ruven did not reply, only nodded once in acknowledgment before stepping away, followed closely by two of the royal guard, leaving Taegan and Zorvut alone in the courtyard with one guard remaining, standing a polite distance behind where they sat. They sat in awkward silence for a moment, then Taegan offered,

"Shall we have lunch?"

Zorvut agreed, so they made their way to the dining hall, still in silence. Taegan found that while the emotions radiating from the pinprick of their bond in the back of his head were familiar, they were not as exact as he would have expected—while he could tell that Zorvut was feeling tense, he could not discern anything more precise, and his face remained largely unreadable. Before they entered the dining hall, he paused and turned to look up at the orc.

"Are you all right?" he asked simply, unsure of what else to say. He could feel a bit of surprise and a tinge of fondness from him at the words.

"Yes," he replied. "Only, it's strange to watch them go and not know when I might see any of them again."

That, at least, Taegan could understand. As they sat down next to each other for a light meal, he found himself wondering about the relationship between Zorvut and his family, but couldn't find the words to phrase his questions without sounding invasive or insensitive. He ruminated over his thoughts, and could feel Zorvut's hesitance over his quiet reflection. By the time he was done eating, the awkwardness of their silence was growing unbearable.

"Did you ever get a full tour of the castle?" Taegan blurted out, finally breaking the silence as a servant cleared away their dishes.

"No, I didn't," Zorvut answered.

"I'll have my attendant give you the full tour, then," he said, standing up and clapping his hands twice—one of the kitchen workers hurried over to him. "Will you have Aerik sent to me in the foyer?"

"Yes, my prince," the man replied, and left the dining hall as swiftly as he had approached.

"Come," Taegan said, beckoning Zorvut to follow.

"You have plans?" Zorvut asked, following. Taegan hesitated—mostly he did not want to be alone with the orc any longer.

"Yes," he said quickly, "I intend to keep working in the archery range. My skills on horseback have been lacking."

Again, the words seemed to pique Zorvut's interest, but he did not comment and only nodded in acceptance. The dining hall was just down a hallway from the main entrance, and they paused in the foyer to wait for Aerik who arrived momentarily from a servant's entrance—though he looked as unruffled as ever, he had come more quickly than Taegan had expected. He hoped the relief he felt upon seeing the other elf was not as apparent to Zorvut as it felt to him.

"My prince," Aerik said, bowing his head respectfully. "You summoned me?"

"Yes, I was hoping you could give Zorvut a full tour of the castle," he said. "I'll be at the archery range."

"Of course," the attendant replied as smoothly as if he had already known exactly what Taegan would ask of him. He turned to look at Zorvut, nodding at him as well. "If you would come with me, Prince Zorvut?"

They both paused at that—though it was truly his title now, Taegan had never referred to him that way. *Prince Zorvut.* Whatever emotion it elicited in Zorvut was unreadable to Taegan.

"Thank you," Zorvut replied simply, and looked back at Taegan. "I will join you later, then."

"Of course," Taegan agreed, and watched them go, Aerik's voice echoing through the hall for a moment as he began to explain the castle's layout and history. Then, he turned and made his way back out onto the field.

The archery range was beginning to feel like the only place where Taegan could make any sense of the world. The tension of the bow string, the familiar whistle and snap of the arrows—these were all things he knew and understood. So he had his horse saddled and went for a brief ride around the castle grounds before returning to the range, focusing only on his craft: the horse and his bow.

He had been at it for a few hours, his muscles burning with exertion and his tunic damp with sweat, when he leapt off his horse to retrieve his arrows and noticed Aerik and Zorvut approaching from the direction of the castle. Taegan raised a hand in greeting, and Aerik's head bobbed in acknowledgment.

"Forgive the interruption, my prince," he said as they came within earshot. "I have given Prince Zorvut a tour of the castle, and have been showing him the gardens and grounds."

"I can show him the archery range, then," Taegan said, catching his breath and slinging his bow across his back. Behind him, Moonlight whickered nervously as they approached—glancing back, he could see her eyes trained on Zorvut. He could feel discomfort coming from Zorvut through the bond, noticing the horse's fear—now that they were closer, his emotions were harder to ignore. Sighing, he patted the mare's neck to calm her.

"I don't mean to interrupt you," Zorvut said, eyeing him up and down.

"No, I'd be happy to show you," Taegan interjected quickly, and waved Aerik away. "I spend most of my time here. No one is better suited to give you the tour of it than me." Zorvut watched Aerik step back politely and acquiesced with a nod of his head.

"Then let me help you get your arrows first," he said, and approached the target. They made quick work of retrieving all the practice arrows, and Taegan deftly placed them back in his quiver before grabbing his horse's lead and walking out toward the open green.

The archery range had a standard practice area, where straw targets lined the wall and most of the spare equipment was stored in a small shed. This was where Aerik and Zorvut had approached, but there was little of note otherwise. The bulk of the range was an open field, then a full mile of wooded paths.

"The field is best for flying targets, though it requires a partner," Taegan explained as they walked—Moonlight had balked for the first few steps, but the longer they walked together, the more she relaxed. Zorvut was pointedly ignoring her, which seemed to help her settle, his gaze alternating between Taegan and the places he was pointing. "Occasionally we would perform battlefield simulations here, but we have a larger field on the other side of the castle that's better suited for large-scale practice."

"Aerik showed me the other training grounds," Zorvut replied.

They walked from the field to the entrance of the wooded path. "Is this part of it, too?" Zorvut asked, trepidation and surprise coming from him.

"It is," Taegan answered, stepping into the shade. "This is my favorite part. The paths go on for a mile. There are targets set up on trees and in the brush, which are changed out weekly. There are some enchanted moving targets as well, to help simulate a hunt."

"What game do you hunt?"

"Deer and boar, mostly. But I like the challenge of smaller game as well, and fowl."

As they walked along the main path, Taegan could see a faint glimmer in the air from the corner of his eye—he drew his bow quickly, startling Zorvut, but the glimmer burst into a shower of sparks as his arrow soared true, pinning the enchanted paper to a towering oak tree with a resounding thunk.

"Good shot," Zorvut said, eyebrows raised.

"Thank you," Taegan replied, a satisfied smile on his lips. Zorvut held out one of his hands.

"May I?" he asked. Taegan hesitated, then handed him the bow and an arrow—though it was a longbow, it was comically small in his much larger hands. Zorvut pulled the bowstring carefully, getting a feel for its weight, then glanced about as they walked. He drew the bow, and Taegan could see his eye trained on a small target nestled in the crook of a tree branch, partly hidden.

*Thwack!* The arrow sped toward its target and pierced it cleanly through—not quite the exact center, but it was a tricky angle. This time, Taegan's eyebrows rose in surprise.

"Good shot," he echoed as Zorvut handed him the bow back.

"I prefer the greatsword, myself," Zorvut replied, glancing up at the target. "But I've been trained in most weapons."

"You're called the Relentless for a reason, I'm sure," Taegan said, and a faint tendril of pride drifted from the bond, like smoke from a candle. "I may not look it, but I am an accomplished warrior in my own right."

"You look it," Zorvut remarked, eyeing him again. This time, the heat that coursed through the bond was unmistakable. "If we had met on the battlefield, I think we would have been quite evenly matched." Taegan chuckled at that, a bitter laugh.

"I could take you out in one shot if you were a good distance away," he said. "But if it were in close quarters, I'd say you would have had a significant advantage." Somehow, this only seemed to cause a spike in the desire smoldering in the back of his head. He glanced up at Zorvut, who was watching him intently. "Do you enjoy thinking of how we might have killed each other?"

"No," he replied, stepping closer to Taegan, closing the space between them so they were mere inches apart. "But you are confident, and strong, and proud. That is what attracts me." Carefully, he lifted his hand to cup Taegan's cheek—his thumb and first two fingers were all it took to encompass the side of his face. Heat sparked between them at the contact, and Taegan found himself leaning into Zorvut's hand despite himself.

The orc leaned down slightly toward his face, but Taegan turned away quickly—he clasped his hand over Zorvut's, though, maintaining the contact on his skin even as he turned away. He could feel his cheeks burning red-hot, desire still coursing through him in spite of the confusion his reaction elicited from Zorvut.

"Will you join me for a bath?" he asked, unable to meet Zorvut's gaze. He wondered if the orc could feel his heart pounding in his chest from this close, if his conflicting feelings were as obvious to him as they felt.

"Yes," Zorvut said softly after just a beat of hesitation, and allowed himself to be led by the hand back out onto the field and toward the castle.

When they reached their quarters, Aerik was waiting outside, sitting in his usual spot. He stood to greet them, but Taegan waved him away quickly.

"Leave us," he said, and wordlessly Aerik nodded and walked down the spiral staircase. They entered the room and Taegan locked the door behind them. A warm bath had already been drawn for them, as he typically enjoyed a bath after spending time at the archery range. His bathroom was lavish, with a deep pool built into the stone floor, so there would be plenty of room for the both of them.

Taegan hesitated, first looking at the bath, then glancing back at Zorvut, who was standing in the doorway, seemingly waiting to follow Taegan's lead. He took in a long, steadying breath, and started to undress, his back to Zorvut. His shirt was tossed unceremoniously to the corner, and he peeled down his breeches and kicked them off in the same direction. Then, forcing himself to keep his breathing slow and even, he turned to face his husband.

Zorvut's gaze was trained on him hungrily, and the heat of arousal coursing between them quickly brought Taegan's already-aching cock to full attention. As Zorvut moved closer to him, he took a step back, the warm water splashing around his ankles as he stepped in.

"Join me?" he said, and watched as Zorvut began to undress. The fine maroon tunic was unlaced quickly and pulled over his head, but he glanced back at Taegan as his fingers hovered over the button of his pants.

Taegan pushed the thought of their first night together out of his mind, and instead raised a quizzical eyebrow. At that, Zorvut smirked faintly, and removed his pants as well. His arousal had already been apparent under his clothes, but the sight of it still made Taegan's heart skip a beat—he tamped down the burgeoning nervousness it elicited in him, and instead held out his hand to lead Zorvut into the bath.

Their eyes met as they entered the water, comfortably warm and lightly scented. Flickering candlelight glinted off the surface of it as they moved, and it struck Taegan that there was something decidedly romantic about the moment. As if sharing his thoughts, Zorvut released his hand and took him into his arms.

The strength and heat of his embrace made Taegan squeeze his eyes shut, his heart pounding—even through the arousal he felt a similar uncertainty coming from Zorvut, so he raised his arms in turn and wrapped them as far around Zorvut's torso as he could reach. They each took in a few long, slow breaths, and he could feel more than hear Zorvut faintly murmur, "Show me what you want. I don't want to hurt you."

Taegan pulled back slightly so he could look at Zorvut's face. There was an earnest determination to his gaze that had not been there the night they had met. He pulled his arms away, instead placing his hands over Zorvut's and guiding them along his body, sliding from his ribs up his chest and shoulders. Letting his hands fall away, he closed his eyes as Zorvut touched him, lightly smoothing his hands up his shoulders and neck, then trailing back down, gingerly brushing over his nipples, abs, and hips. His body burned with heat in the wake of his touch, and he could feel himself dripping with arousal. Zorvut's hands moved away, and there was a slight splash—he laughed, opening his eyes, as Zorvut began to rinse him off.

Taegan reached over to retrieve a soft cloth and soap, and carefully they washed each other. The intimacy of it fueled his desire nearly as much as the thick muscle under his fingers as Taegan ran his hands over Zorvut's body. He hesitated as his fingers trailed down Zorvut's defined abs—he could feel his muscles tense under his touch, and somehow the hitch in Zorvut's breath gave him enough courage to move his hand lower down and touch the massive cock with one long, slow stroke. A low, soft noise rumbled through Zorvut's chest—and he could *feel* the pleasure course through the bond, as recognizably as if it were his own cock being stroked.

He had not expected that. Zorvut's eyes opened—he had not realized they were closed—and met his gaze.

"The bed might be more comfortable," he found himself saying breathlessly, and Zorvut nodded. In one swift movement, Taegan realized Zorvut had picked him up and was carrying him, and the sound escaping him was a whimper, helpless and needy. The display of strength went straight to his cock, his arousal unbearable with the flood of desire pouring from the bond.

Zorvut carried him to the bed effortlessly, then paused as if thinking. Taegan opened his mouth to speak, but before he could, Zorvut was shifting him, easily lifting him higher so his legs straddled the orc's massive shoulders, his arms curling around his back.

"What are you—?" Taegan started to ask, only to trail off wordlessly as Zorvut pulled him close and took his cock into his mouth. There was a flash of fear as he felt Zorvut's tusks press against his hips, but it was quickly forgotten—his mouth was hot and wet and Zorvut sucked him greedily, and the pleasure that coursed through his body echoed through the bond as they both felt the same sensation. He felt the orc groan around his cock, and the feedback loop of pleasure was so intense he could barely stop himself from coming right then.

"Wait—ahh!" he gasped, clutching desperately at Zorvut's hair, one arm wrapping around the orc's neck. The pleasure wracking his body was unlike anything he had ever felt before, like an electric current coursing through both of them and amplifying each sensation to dizzying heights.

"Come," he felt Zorvut's muffled growl around him, his tongue moving insistently against the head of his cock, and that was all it took. Taegan stifled a cry as he came hard, feeling Zorvut groan in satisfaction around his cock as he drank each spurt, his hips thrusting of their own accord into his mouth. For a moment, all he could see were stars.

When he could see again, gasping and panting, Zorvut was sitting on the bed and had lowered him to sit in his lap, watching him carefully. There was desire flashing in his golden eyes, but it seemed carefully tempered as Zorvut held him.

"I want to be inside you," he said, his voice a low rumble echoing deep in his chest. Wordlessly, Taegan nodded, already feeling how slick he was with arousal. Whatever fear still lingered in his chest was far overpowered with lust, with a burning need to be fucked by his massive cock.

But even with his permission, Zorvut was still careful and slow. He leaned back, pulling Taegan with him, so that he lounged on the bed and Taegan straddled his waist, letting his hands trail down Taegan's sides first, then taking firm handfuls of his ass. Spreading him apart, he gingerly pressed a finger against Taegan's aching hole—it slid in effortlessly, eliciting a soft moan from each of them.

"It's true, then," Zorvut murmured as he quickly added a second finger, Taegan squeezing his eyes shut in pleasure. "What they say about elves. Gods, you're wet."

"What do they say about elves?" Taegan asked breathlessly, rocking his hips against Zorvut's hand, his free hand bracing against his hip. He knew, but he wanted to hear Zorvut say it.

"They say elf assholes are just as tight and wet as elf pussies," the orc said, meeting Taegan's gaze hungrily. His cock twitched with renewed interest at the filthy words, already hard again and aching for more. "Fuck, I can't believe how wet you are." Taegan gasped as a third finger worked inside him, stretching him wide, knowing his cock would stretch him wider still.

"Fuck me, then," Taegan urged him, unable to bear the thought of waiting any longer. Zorvut shook his head, his fingers still moving insistently inside him. "*Please*," he whined, and he could feel Zorvut's cock twitch where it was pressed against his belly. This seemed to be all the convincing he needed, as Zorvut pulled his hand away, Taegan keening at the sudden emptiness inside him. But it was soon replaced with the pressure of the head of Zorvut's cock pressing against his entrance, coated in his slick.

"You move," Zorvut said, the same hesitance creeping through the bond again underneath the feedback loop of pleasure. "I don't want to hurt you." Taegan nodded, and slowly lowered himself onto his cock. He sucked in a sharp breath, already feeling the burning stretch of its girth, bigger than anything he'd taken before. Zorvut groaned, feeling his pain even as Taegan felt his pleasure. Taegan took a steadying breath, and pushed down a bit further, taking in the whole head. Zorvut pulled one hand away from Taegan's hips and began to stroke his cock, murmuring in encouragement. Pleasure coursed through him, drowning out the discomfort, and Taegan pushed down a little further each time he thrust into Zorvut's hand. Soon he had half the cock inside him, unbearably full yet desperate for more.

Their movements were slow and careful, Zorvut remaining perfectly still as Taegan rocked back and forth against him, yet even so it felt like only a moment before the familiar pressure welling up in Taegan's belly was pushing him to the brink. He tried to speak, but the orgasm was already pulsing through him, and all that escaped him was a wordless moan. His body clenched hard around Zorvut, who groaned and finally moved his own hips, fucking him through his orgasm and making him cry out in ecstasy.

In a few quick thrusts, Zorvut was coming inside him—he could feel the hot pulse filling him, then his cock pulled out, a gush of liquid spilling out of him as it did. He gasped at the sudden emptiness, then at the hot stripes of come shooting across his torso, streaking his chin and throat and fully coating his belly. Much as he yearned to feel the warm, sticky fluid inside him, there was something erotic about the orc coming on his body, marking him. Claiming him.

For a long moment, they remained motionless, panting and catching their breath in the afterglow of their consummation. Taegan watched Zorvut's face as the pleasure washing through them slowly receded through the bond, settling into a comfortable tingle. The orc's eyes slid open and met his gaze. An unexpected sense of accomplishment welled up in him, and a slight grin played at his lips which Zorvut hesitantly returned.

Straightening his back, he swung a leg over Zorvut's waist and slid off the bed, standing shakily. He was covered in sweat and come and slick—a much smaller puddle of his own come was splattered across Zorvut's abs. There was some definite soreness as he stood, but not as much as he might have expected. Zorvut watched him carefully, as if worried he might collapse, but Taegan met his gaze evenly and held out his hand.

"Will you join me for a bath?" he asked, then added, "Again?" At that, Zorvut chuckled, and wordlessly took his hand.

# Chapter Six

Once they had jumped over the first hurdle, it felt like the floodgates had opened, and Taegan found he could think of nothing else. Even just the half of Zorvut's cock that he had been able to take in had been such an exquisite fullness that he was certain he could never be satisfied with anything smaller again. The feedback loop their bond created only multiplied his desire, and the moment one of them first started to think of it, soon they would be fucking no matter what they had been doing before.

The next day, Zorvut met with the tailor again to choose some fabrics for more shirts; Taegan was so aroused at the sight of the different silks and cottons being draped over his muscled torso that he excused himself after only a few minutes, returning to his room to touch himself desperately. The thought of Zorvut feeling his pleasure and desire yet unable to do anything about it only made him harder—it took less than ten minutes for the door to burst open, and Zorvut stormed inside, lifting him onto the bed and pulling his clothes off. He did not bother with his hands this time, but despite how roughly he handled Taegan, he was still careful not to push his cock inside further than Taegan had taken it the night before.

"Harder," Taegan whimpered, but Zorvut ignored him, setting a rapid but shallow pace that still left him a trembling, sticky mess.

Then they had gone to Taegan's private study, so he could make good on his promise to read to Zorvut. He could sense the orc's gaze on him, hot and hungry, and he made it through maybe two paragraphs before they pushed aside their books and Zorvut bent him over the desk. But Zorvut was *still* maddeningly cautious, and Taegan *knew* he could take more of his cock, desperate to feel it filling him to the base. Still, with the bond amplifying their emotions and sensations, it only took a few moments before they were both coming. Then they had needed a bath, and never quite got back to the books.

Once, when they were face to face and Zorvut was moving slowly, cautiously inside him, he had leaned down as if to kiss Taegan. He had turned his face away quickly without thinking—as foolish as it seemed, somehow it felt too intimate to kiss him. Zorvut hesitated at the rejection, and when they were finished, he went silently to the bathroom to clean up, leaving Taegan alone.

It *was* foolish, he told himself, unsure if the shame he felt was coming from him or the bond; Zorvut was his husband, after all, and if he could have the orc inside him, why couldn't he kiss him as well? Zorvut had left their quarters quietly after that, and Taegan was not sure where he went, but did not see him again until after the evening meal. He feared Zorvut might try to sleep on the floor again after that, but luckily, he still came to bed.

Things went on this way for the first week—and when they were not fucking or wanting to fuck, they were mostly apart. It was easier to ignore his conflicting feelings, so Taegan spent most of his free time at the archery range. He was not sure where Zorvut went or what he did when they parted ways, but he tried not to think about it, tried not to let himself feel the beginnings of arousal that would inevitably drive him to hastily put away his equipment and find Zorvut waiting for him outside their quarters. That happened more often than he would have liked.

After the first week or so, though, he thought he was getting a hold on the bond. With some effort, he found he could mostly block out emotions coming from Zorvut, though he was not sure how successful his attempts at masking his own emotions from the bond might have been. Zorvut did not mention one way or the other, but the better Taegan got at regulating the bond, the less frenzied and desperate their arousal became. He was even able to give a distinct sensation of *later* when he felt Zorvut wanting him at an inopportune time—and a few days later, was surprised to feel that same thought of *later* coming from Zorvut, as he was daydreaming absentmindedly in the bath.

In spite of everything, he thought things were going better than either of them had expected. For that, if nothing else, he was grateful.

Over an evening meal later that week, King Ruven asked them to join him on a hunt the next day.

"Perhaps Taegan has told you that hunting season has begun," he said to Zorvut, who nodded politely. "This is the best time of year for hunting elk. I plan to set out with a small party tomorrow morning, and would be pleased if both of you joined us."

"Of course," Taegan replied, feeling Zorvut's gaze shift to him. He turned to meet the orc's eyes. "We would both love to join, yes?"

There was a slight flash of hesitance which Taegan felt Zorvut quickly dampen, and the orc nodded. "Yes," he agreed simply.

"Excellent," Ruven said. "We set out at dawn."

Zorvut had the foresight to have kept his horse, as none of the many horses they had were large enough for him to safely ride—his own horse was so large that a special stall had to be added onto the stable just for him. Taegan had only ever seen the stallion in passing, but when two stable boys led the saddled horses out to them as they gathered in the courtyard at sunrise the next morning, he watched the impressive beast trot out eagerly, his own mare following more cautiously.

"What is your horse called?" he asked as Zorvut took the horse's reins, running a hand along his snout with a surprising fondness. The stallion snorted, tossing his head—he was a jet black but with a vivid splash of gray just above his hooves that extended up his legs, as if he had walked through a puddle of silver.

"Graksh't," Zorvut replied, the harsh orcish language taking Taegan by surprise—he had not heard Zorvut speak it since the day they had gone to the orc encampment the night after their wedding. "It means... well, something like 'champion.'"

"Graksh't," Taegan repeated, though even as he tried to get his mouth around the words, he could tell he was not saying it correctly. He took his own horse's reins, noting her snowy white mane had been braided just the way he liked. "My horse is named Moonlight. I've had her since I was a child. She was a gift from my father."

"Graksh't is the son of my father's most prized mare," Zorvut replied.

Something about the conversation felt like pulling teeth, but luckily the hunting party interrupted before he had to think of a response. King Ruven rode up to them, somehow still looking regal even in his leather hunting gear.

"Ready?" he asked, and they followed as he led the way out of the city gates.

It was a good two hour's ride through the woods and into the grassy hills where the best game could historically be found, but the trip was always a pleasant one, especially with the sun coming up on the horizon, sending streaks of morning light across the misty hills. King Ruven and his hunting party rode a bit ahead of them; the same three elves had joined him on his hunting trips for many years. One was Ruven's cousin and the two others a baron and baroness couple, who owned a large plot of land just outside the city walls where they would often hunt smaller game in the off seasons.

Seeing the four of them riding up ahead with the sun rising to the east filled Taegan with a strange sense of nostalgia—when he was very young, his other father would be with them, often riding alongside a small Taegan on his old pony behind the others as well, pointing out landmarks and rock formations so they would not lose their way and quizzing Taegan on the names of plants they encountered.

Zorvut glanced at him, and he realized his nostalgia and that familiar tinge of sadness at the thought of Papa had leaked through the bond to him, but he couldn't quite bring himself to explain. Instead, he pointed out one of the familiar rock formations on the horizon.

"We've always called this rock the crone, since it looks like a figure hunched over," he said, feeling Zorvut's gaze follow his finger to the shape in the distance. "I don't know if it has an official name, but it's what my fathers would call it every time we passed it. I always knew that when we saw the crone, we had left the borders of the capital."

As they traveled, he pointed out more of the familiar landmarks, but they became few and far between as they went further into the forest and the trees became more dense, soon blotting out most of the morning sunlight and limiting the range of their vision. Once they were in the darkened, shaded woods, Ruven turned back to look at them.

"Quiet, now," he said in a hushed tone, and Taegan nodded, Zorvut following suit. When he turned back around, Taegan leaned closer to Zorvut.

"This time of year, the elk are migrating from the grasslands through the forest," he added in a whisper. "It's more challenging to hunt them in the forest, but he likes the challenge. Depending on how it goes, we might push through to the fields or see what we can find here." Zorvut nodded, glancing around, but did not respond.

They made their way quietly through the woods, the horses ambling along the dirt path they had followed many times before. After a little ways, one of the barons raised his hand and they paused, listening intently. He waved and pointed to the left, and the four elves dismounted quickly, drawing their bows.

Taegan hesitated, unsure how quietly Zorvut could dismount, so he held out his hand in a halting gesture and remained on his horse. They watched the four elves creep into the woods, and soon could no longer spot them. Taegan held his breath as they waited, straining his ears for the telltale snap of an arrow being fired.

But the sound he heard was a twig snapping, then a familiar bellowing of a bull elk.

"Damn!" the baron shouted as the elk galloped away—Taegan only caught a glimpse of him through the trees, and his father approached with a chagrined expression, followed by the other three. As they mounted their horses, King Ruven looked back at the two of them waiting.

"Good call," he said, gesturing toward Taegan. "I don't think we'll have much luck in the woods today. Let's push through to the grassland. Once we spot the herd, we'll split up."

Zorvut nodded in agreement, and they followed the four elves through the winding path until eventually the light began to break through the canopy again, first an occasional dappled patch of sun, then a more diffused brightness as the trees became more sparse and spread out. Soon, the forest gave way to rolling grassy hills, and as they ascended the initial peak, Zorvut leaned over to Taegan.

"I can hear the herd," he whispered. His soft voice sent a shiver up Taegan's spine that he did his best to ignore. "Just below this hill, I think."

Sure enough, as they reached the top of the hillside and could look down to the sloping valley below, the herd of elk was visible, grazing and meandering through the field. King Ruven gestured for them to draw closer, and they huddled together for a hushed conversation.

"Daven and I will take the center," he said, pointing toward the herd as he spoke. "Taegan, you and Zorvut flank them on the right, and Bela and Yulen can approach from the left. Do you see the big fellow with the vine stuck to his antlers? Let's try and get him away from the rest."

The group nodded in agreement, and they split up, Taegan and Zorvut descending the hill from the right to swing around the gathered herd. The large bull elk Ruven had pointed out was nearer to the center, lazily following a female as she grazed. There was a slight opening they should be able to drive through to cut them off from the rest of the herd, and Taegan first met Zorvut's eyes, then pointed at the gap. The orc nodded in recognition. They waited, watching the distant figures of Ruven and the rest of the hunting party getting into position, then Daven waved his arm and they galloped toward the herd.

The frightened bellowing of the elk on the outskirts of the herd soon sent most of them dashing away, but Taegan was able to cut them off, preventing the bull and the unlucky female from following the herd. They made a few nervous leaps toward the opposite side of the hill, but the baron and baroness blocked their way, one of the horses rearing back and sending the female elk skittering away in fear.

"Quickly!" he could hear Ruven exclaim as they circled the two elk. The bull pranced between them, and Taegan could see it glancing about, looking for an opening.

"Don't let him get away!" he exclaimed, but it was too late—the bull was charging toward the hill, trying to break through between Ruven and Daven's horses. They couldn't close the gap between them quick enough and the elk went dashing past, though Ruven loosed an arrow and caught it in its front leg, causing it to stumble and screech before continuing its mad dash.

The thunderous gallop of Zorvut and his massive horse were close behind, and he streaked past the others in pursuit. Taegan dashed after them, but the sheer size of Graksh't meant his stride was nearly double that of Moonlight's, outpacing her easily when they were at a full gallop.

Zorvut came up alongside the elk as effortlessly as if he were approaching another horse, and Taegan kept as close behind as he could to prevent it from turning to the side or going back the way it came. He watched as Zorvut drew his bow, his measured movements almost in slow motion compared to the frantic movement of the elk, and as soon as it turned its head to look at the orc with its eyes rolling in terror, he loosed the arrow which drove right through the creature's skull. This time, the elk made no noise, but simply crumpled to the ground, dead in an instant.

"Gods!" he heard Daven exclaim from behind them as the four elves caught up. They circled their prey as Zorvut dismounted and went to retrieve his arrow. He pulled Ruven's from its foreleg as well, handing it back to the king.

"Incredible shot," Ruven said as he looked the beast over, looking equal parts impressed and shocked. "I've never seen someone keep pace with an elk that size before. Maybe I should look into getting a bigger horse."

Zorvut chuckled, glancing away. "Thank you," he said. "It does help to have a larger horse."

Bela, the baroness, began to unpack a small wooden frame from her saddlebags. The carved pieces fit together to create a tiny sleigh that she held in both hands, but she whispered an incantation and it glowed with a reddish light, magically growing in size until it was large enough to haul the carcass of the elk. "Well, let's get it up the hill," she said, and they made their way back toward the forest with their prize.

At the top of the hill, they decided to build a fire and butcher the elk, making it easier to carry with them and get a taste of it while it was freshest.

"Please, allow me," Zorvut said, drawing his blade, and no one could bring themselves to protest. He made quick work of it, cleanly removing the legs and gutting it while the others built a campfire. One of its hind legs was set to roast over the flame while the rest was strapped onto the cart. Bela moved her hands over it, murmuring a different incantation this time, before declaring, "That should keep it cold until we return home."

The hot, freshly roasted meat was passed around, each of them taking a bite, enjoying the tender smokiness. When they had eaten their fill, they headed back toward the woods to return to the capital. The sun was nearing the middle of the sky, so it would still be early afternoon when they arrived back at the castle.

As they rode, Taegan glanced over at Zorvut next to him. He seemed more comfortable and relaxed in the saddle than Taegan thought he had ever seen him before. Zorvut noticed his glance and looked over at him, their eyes meeting for a brief moment. There was a flash of something like fondness in the bond before Taegan looked away.

"This has been a pleasant trip," he said, and though he was not looking, he could feel Zorvut smile.

"It has," he agreed. "I have... enjoyed spending the day with you, Taegan."

A faint shiver of excitement shot down his spine. It was the first time he had heard Zorvut refer to him by his name, at least since they had said their vows to each other. He looked back over to him to see Zorvut watching him closely, an unexpected tenderness in his golden-yellow eyes. Taegan's mouth opened to speak, but he could not find the words—he wasn't even sure what it was he wanted to say.

"As have I," he stammered, unable to come up with anything else. A tiny smirk played at Zorvut's lips, and Taegan glanced away quickly, embarrassed. "We should take trips like this often, to get out of the castle."

"We should," Zorvut agreed, and his horse trotted a few steps closer to Taegan's. They walked side by side for a while, in a silence that became more bearable the longer it went on.

# Chapter Seven

After a month, they had largely settled into a new normal. Having an orc in the castle was no longer a strange novelty for the staff and servants, and while some of the elves still seemed a bit uncomfortable around Zorvut, they would at least look at him and speak to him. Taegan found Zorvut to be an early riser and they spent most mornings apart, but would meet in the afternoons in the archery range or the library or his private study. He had been reading to Zorvut, as he had promised, and occasionally would find Zorvut alone in the study with an elven text and a dictionary. For all the stereotypes about orcs being brutish and violent, only caring to pursue knowledge when it would aid in their conquests, Zorvut was proving to be a very thoughtful and eager learner.

Late one afternoon, as they were leaving the castle library with a few scrolls and books, a voice called out from behind them.

"Prince Taegan," the male voice echoed through the quiet room, and they turned to see Kelvhan walking toward him. Irritation bristled at the sight of him, an echo of their last conversation despite the time they had spent apart, but Taegan suppressed it quickly, not wanting Zorvut to sense anything at all about him.

"Kelvhan," he replied dryly. The other elf bowed his head in respect, but kept his gaze trained on Taegan. Zorvut glanced at him, then back over at Taegan with an uncertain expression. "Zorvut, this is Kelvhan, a warlock in service of the library."

"Forgive the intrusion, my prince," Kelvhan continued before Zorvut could reply. "I was hoping to speak to you in private."

At that, Taegan hesitated. While he truly did not want to talk to Kelvhan, if he refused, it might appear more suspicious than if he agreed. He sighed and gave a terse nod of agreement.

"I'll meet you in the dining hall for dinner," he said to Zorvut.

"Let me take those back to your study, then," the orc replied, gesturing at the books he carried, which Taegan handed over with a faint simmer of affection bubbling through his frustration at the offer. He looked back over to Kelvhan as Zorvut turned to go, noting that the disdain on the other elf's face was apparent.

"Well?" he asked expectantly after a beat of silence.

"Come with me," Kelvhan said, turning away. This time, Taegan was positive the flash of irritation he felt at Kelvhan's purposely vague words had carried through the bond, and he could feel a faint mixture of confusion and concern coming from Zorvut in return. *Later*, he thought, and did his best to close off his end of the bond for now. Kelvhan led him to a quiet corner near the back of the library, where some of the oldest tomes were kept and it was unlikely anyone would overhear them.

"Taegan," he said when they were alone, turning to face him.

"*Prince* Taegan," he interrupted, and Kelvhan scowled at the correction.

"Please don't be like this," he countered, his voice a frustrated hiss. "I just wanted to talk to you."

"I'm listening," he retorted. Kelvhan sucked in a long breath before continuing in a measured, forced tone.

"I have been thinking about what you said the last time we spoke," he said slowly. "And I truly think we could make this work. Taegan, I..." His voice hesitated there, and he looked away. "Taegan, I miss you. I miss what we had. You're too good for—for *him*, for an orc. Your marriage is only a symbol, nothing more, and that doesn't have to change. But we can still be together, we *should* still be together. Elves should be with elves."

"I thought I made my decision clear," Taegan snapped, scowling. "Kelvhan, what you ask of me is impossible."

"It's *not*," he insisted. "Monarchs have had secret relationships since the beginning of time. Everyone knows political marriages have no expectation of love. No one could fault you for this."

He reached to grab Taegan's hand; he pulled away, but Kelvhan's grasp was firm. The sensation of his soft, warm skin against Taegan's hand was so intimate that for one uncertain moment, he considered it—as well as things were going with Zorvut, how long could it last? They were so different, and Kelvhan was so familiar—

What was he thinking? He yanked his hand away, anger and shame flooding him for even entertaining the thought.

"I will *not* endanger the peace treaty this way," he growled, struggling to keep his voice quiet yet stern. "Kelvhan, I don't think you understand why I did this in the first place. My father worked too hard for too long for me to put it on the line for—for—for what? A handful of secret meetings? A year together? No, a lifetime of unity isn't worth giving up for you, for anyone."

Kelvhan's face had gone from ghostly white to a furious red, and he opened his mouth to protest, but Taegan did not let him.

"You forget yourself," he continued, jabbing a finger toward him as he stepped away. His voice was rising with anger, and he was sure everyone else in the library could hear him clear as day—part of him hoped they did. "I am the prince, and the next time you speak to me this way, it will be your last moment in this castle. Do not approach me about this again, do you understand?"

Kelvhan stared at him for a long moment, his mouth a firm line but rage blazing in his eyes, until finally he looked away and swallowed hard. "I understand," he whispered, barely audible, and without staying to hear if he had anything else to say, Taegan turned to go, his footsteps echoing loudly through the library as he stormed out.

Without thinking, he returned to his room, wanting to be alone, but Zorvut was already there and waiting for him, a concerned look on his face as Taegan shoved the door open.

"What's wrong?" Zorvut asked, standing up to meet him. Taegan turned away, feeling his cheeks flush.

"Nothing," he said, the word coming out as a hoarse whisper. He cleared his throat, then added, "I... I do not like that man."

"I could tell," Zorvut replied slowly, the uncertainty apparent in his voice and his face. "You were certainly... feeling uncomfortable. I was worried about you."

Taegan knew the words were meant to assuage him, but for some reason anger spiked anew in his chest.

"Perhaps it would be best if I kept the bond more closed off," he snapped, unable to meet the orc's gaze. "I would not want to bother you with my unnecessary thoughts." He could feel a steady stream of confusion coming from Zorvut, but he squeezed his eyes shut, imagining them as iron vaults blocking him off from their connection—he heard Zorvut gasp, and opened his eyes to see him instinctively reaching for the back of his neck. Though he felt a sharp pinprick of panic coming from Zorvut, he must have been successful in closing his own end of the bond.

"I didn't know you could..." Zorvut stammered, trailing off before turning away from Taegan. "I'm sorry. I didn't mean to anger you."

"You didn't anger me!" Taegan shouted, but the petulance in his tone was painful even to his own ears, and he clenched his fists before turning away as well and repeating in a forced tone, "You didn't anger me."

"I'll go," Zorvut said simply, and pushed past Taegan and was out the door before he could react. Taegan stood alone and motionless in the middle of the room for a long moment, frustrated tears burning at his eyes that he refused to shed. Finally, he picked up one of the books Zorvut had brought back for him and sat down to read, though his gaze lingered on the same paragraph without comprehension for the remainder of the afternoon. When he finally felt calm enough to discern his own emotions from Zorvut's, he could only sense a faint sadness coming from the orc.

Zorvut did not join them for dinner, and when King Ruven asked about it, Taegan stammered out something about him not feeling well and staying behind. The king seemed to sense his uncertainty, and did not press him on the matter.

After the meal, he still could not focus on the book he had been trying to read, so he drew a bath to try and relax a bit before bed. Much to his chagrin, he heard the door opening as Zorvut returned to their room while he was still in the bath. When he padded back into the bedroom in only his nightclothes, he found that the orc had stripped a blanket off the bed and laid down on the floor, the way he had their first night together.

"Zorvut," Taegan said softly—the sight of his husband on the floor hurt him in a way he had not expected. "Why don't you come to bed?"

But Zorvut's eyes remained firmly shut—he was certain Zorvut was still awake—and he did not respond.

"Please?" he asked, but when he was again met with silence, he sighed and blew out the candles on his side of the room. After what felt like an hour, he heard

Zorvut shift and sit up, and the candlelight on that side flickered out as well.

Closing off his end of the bond was a mistake, and it took a conscious effort the next morning to let Zorvut back in—or, at least, he hoped it was successful, but the orc was distant and avoidant, already gone by the time Taegan woke in the morning. He did not join him for lunch, and could not be found in the usual places they spent their afternoons. When he asked Aerik if he had seen him, the attendant advised him that Zorvut had asked him to saddle his horse first thing in the morning, so he expected he might still be riding if he had not returned.

"His horse?" Taegan asked sharply, suddenly worried. "Did he take anything with him?"

"No, my prince, only a bow and quiver. I thought perhaps he was getting in some early morning target practice. Is there cause for concern?" Aerik replied, though his face was as carefully neutral as ever.

"No, no," Taegan muttered, waving his hand dismissively. "You're right. He wanted to spend the day practicing. I... I forgot he had mentioned it."

The lie seemed painfully obvious, but Aerik only nodded in agreement. "Of course."

When he was alone in his study, he sat down on the floor and closed his eyes, focusing on the point in the back of his head where Zorvut was connected to him. *I'm sorry*, he thought, and let the phrase repeat in his head, trying to think it at the bond, trying to push all his emotions at it, wondering if anything was going through at all. *I'm sorry. I'm sorry.* After a moment, the familiar sense of *later* answered him, and he sighed in relief—it meant that at the very least, Zorvut was safe, and near enough to sense him.

But he was still gone when Taegan met his father in the dining hall for dinner again.

"Still unwell?" Ruven asked as Taegan sat down next to him.

"Yes," Taegan replied with a sigh. He hesitated, then turned to look at his father and continued in a hushed tone. "Could we speak after dinner, in private?"

"Of course," the king said, raising an eyebrow. "You do not need to ask, my son."

He had little appetite and mostly pushed his food around his plate until dinner was over and his father stood, taking a goblet of wine with him, and he followed the king up the spiral staircase to his private study.

"Something is bothering you," Ruven remarked as Taegan closed the door behind him.

"Is it that obvious?" he answered with a groan, sitting down at his father's desk. Ruven stood, taking a sip of his wine, watching him silently from the other side. "I... Well, I wanted to ask for your advice, I suppose."

"Tell me," the king prompted. Taegan was silent, considering his words for a long moment.

"You know I want this to work," he finally said. "Zorvut and I. For the sake of all of us, for you, I want this marriage to work. Things were going better for a little while, but... I don't know. We've been—I've been struggling to connect with him, emotionally."

He paused, but Ruven remained silent, waiting for him to finish. "I don't know how. I feel like I never know the right thing to say to him, and the things I do say, he doesn't react the way I would expect him to. And him, I know there are times he tries to do or say things, *kind* things, to me, but..." He trailed off, unable to find the words, and instead looked helplessly to his father.

"But?" Ruven repeated.

"But... I don't know. I don't react the way I think he wants me to react, either," he stammered. "I don't understand him. Sometimes I don't understand why I feel the way I do, either." At that, Ruven chuckled.

"I think part of you has always been that way," he said wryly, then sighed. "But relationships can be difficult, more so when you're as... different as you and Zorvut are from each other. To be frank, Taegan, it may always be a struggle. I don't know if relating to an orc will ever come easily to us, at least not in this lifetime. We have considered ourselves enemies for generations, and loath as I am to admit it, one peace treaty isn't going to change that overnight."

"Perhaps," Taegan sighed, looking away. He had not expected so hopeless of a response.

"But," Ruven added quickly, sensing his discouragement. "That is not to say you shouldn't try. Haven't you always been one to talk out your feelings, like this?" He gestured between them, and Taegan managed a slight smile, nodding in agreement. "That is what works best for you. But what works best for him? If there is a different avenue that might be more relatable to Zorvut, perhaps that would be a better option for you to try. Other races do not experience the mental bond we do. What might be intuitive for you to use to express yourself is likely completely alien to him. You need to find what is intuitive for him."

"Right," Taegan agreed, his brow furrowed in thought. It seemed obvious now that the king spoke it aloud, but he supposed he had never quite considered it that way. "I'll think on it."

His father came around the desk and patted his shoulder gently. "I can see this is important to you. I have every confidence you can find a solution, and I hope Zorvut is receptive to you. Honestly, I am impressed at how easily he has adapted, so hopefully he wants things to go well between the two of you, too."

He paused, then squeezed Taegan's shoulder. "And if nothing else, I am always here for you. We are in an unprecedented situation, and we may just have to make do with what we get."

"Of course," Taegan murmured in agreement, and he stood. "I appreciate your advice, Father."

He took his leave and went for a walk around the grounds, hoping to spot Zorvut. He and Graksh't would be hard to miss, he was sure, but he had no such luck. It was a pleasantly warm spring day, though, and the fresh air helped clear his head.

They had gotten along well when they had gone on that hunt, he thought, so perhaps another hunting trip could help. If anything, the times they had been outdoors together, alone, had been some of the times they had been most vulnerable with each other; he remembered the day he first showed Zorvut the wooded path in the archery range, how they seemed to communicate best when discussing what was familiar between them—the bow, the sword. There was something there.

After he had walked the grounds, he came back to the cool shade of the castle, and when he arrived back in his room, he could hear that Zorvut had returned and was bathing. He was tempted to join him, but that seemed too presumptuous—instead, he settled into one of his comfy chairs with a book, and waited. Now that they were closer, he could feel Zorvut more closely in his head, though the feelings were muted and weak, as if he were also trying to remain more closed-off to him. It felt like a faint whisper of sadness, so distant he could only hear it when he focused on nothing else.

Eventually, Zorvut emerged from the bath, dressed only in loose breeches, his bare chest still glistening with moisture and his wet hair sticking to his skin. He glanced at Taegan and gave a slight nod of acknowledgment but did not speak, instead going for the wardrobe and pulling out a clean shirt, a dark purple tunic. Desire stirred in Taegan as he watched Zorvut pull the shirt over his head, but he tamped it down.

"I was hoping to speak with you," he said, standing up. Zorvut gestured for him to continue, keeping his back turned. "I was... I wondered if you'd like to come with me on a hunt, just the two of us." He could feel Zorvut hesitate—whatever he had thought to hear from Taegan, it seemed this had not been it. Finally, he turned to meet his gaze.

"Why?" he asked, much more blunt than Taegan expected, and he blinked in surprise.

"Well," he said slowly, trying to gather his thoughts. "I thought it might be nice to get out of the castle for a bit. This time of year, there are giant boars to the south. It might be a decent challenge to take one down."

Zorvut seemed unconvinced, his expression unchanged. Taegan hesitated, then added, "And it would be nice... to spend some time alone with you."

The face Zorvut made as he said it seemed pained, but he sighed and nodded. "All right," he agreed. "When?"

"We could go tomorrow," Taegan said quickly, before Zorvut could change his mind. "It's a few hours' ride, but if we leave in the afternoon, we would arrive in the forest where they live around sunset, when they're most active."

"Sure," Zorvut agreed, giving a terse nod. "We'll go tomorrow." He hesitated, clearly thinking of something and debating whether or not to speak, and he took a step closer to Taegan, looking him carefully in the eye. "Taegan, I don't know what I did yesterday to upset you, and you don't have to tell me," he said quickly, his voice low with emotion. "But, please don't do... *that*, again. It was... uncomfortable."

"I understand," Taegan replied softly, though he was not sure exactly what Zorvut meant. "And I'm sorry. I was frustrated with something else and took it out on you." Zorvut nodded, his shoulders visibly starting to relax, and Taegan took a step closer to him, running his hands up the orc's muscled arms. "Come to bed with me?"

"No," Zorvut replied quickly. He tensed, but did not pull away. "No, not yet, I... Maybe later."

"Okay," Taegan said, stepping back. "Perhaps I can read to you, instead." They were silent for a moment, then Zorvut nodded.

"That sounds nice," he said. They settled into their armchairs, Taegan turning his to face Zorvut, and he read aloud until they left for their evening meal.

# Chapter Eight

The following morning, Taegan made all the arrangements for their trip, and by the early afternoon everything was prepared for them to make the journey to the Silverwood, where giant boar roamed in abundance during the spring and summer. It would be an overnight trip, he explained to Zorvut as they prepared to set out, and they would return the next evening. Graksh't carried some of the heavier camping supplies, while Moonlight carried extra arrows and bedding that did not quite fit in their backpacks.

They set out, Taegan leading the way and Zorvut following quietly. He still seemed tense and distant, but Taegan was just glad he had agreed to come at all. It was a long ride, but a scenic one, and as Taegan pointed out landmarks and villages he felt like he was mostly talking to himself. Zorvut followed a few paces behind him, always within earshot, but never quite side-by-side, although the road was wide enough to allow it.

"That village along the river there is where my father was born," he said, a few hours into their trip. The small fishing village of Pondshear was nestled in between the bend of the river and the foothills of a mountain range. Zorvut glanced over at him, a faint look of surprise crossing over his face.

"The king?" he asked.

"No, my other father," he said, shaking his head. "They met when Papa was a knight." He smiled faintly, remembering the story he had been told a hundred times before. "It caused a big fuss for a prince to want to marry a knight, but he was the prince, and no one could tell him no. And Papa was the greatest swordsman in the royal guard, which was why he came to live in the capital—and, well, this part may have been an embellishment, but they always said that if anyone tried to keep them apart, Papa could cut them down, no matter who they were." He made a slashing motion with one hand, the same way Papa would whenever he told the story.

When he looked back, Zorvut was still peering over at the fishing village, but met his gaze when he noticed Taegan watching him.

"He was a warrior," Zorvut repeated. "Was he slain in battle?"

Taegan flinched at the blunt question. "Yes," he replied. "Almost ten years ago, now." He hesitated, and added, "You may have heard of him, Alain Glynzeiros. He was known for wielding two swords, rather than a sword and shield. He led a battalion into the eastern mountains, hoping to launch a surprise attack on the orc trade post there while the warlord visited, but they were intercepted. They were able to retrieve his body and bring it back for a proper burial, but..." He trailed off. The last part of the story was always the worst to tell.

"Without his arms," Zorvut finished, and Taegan nodded. "Yes, I've heard of him. I had not realized..." He sighed, looking away. From the bond, he could sense something like bitterness. "I'm sure this would not change how you feel, but I wasn't in that battle. I was too young then."

"I know," Taegan said quickly. "We found out after the fact that the warlord was still in Drol Kuggradh with his clan. My father was..." He trailed off, remembering King Ruven's helpless fury after learning their information had been wrong. "Well, he forbade me from training with the sword for a long time after that, which is why I mainly use a bow now."

"Understandable," Zorvut murmured, still not quite meeting his gaze.

There wasn't much more to say on the matter, and they fell into an awkward silence for a moment.

The fishing village disappeared behind a hill as they continued along the winding road.

Before much longer, the tree line of the Silverwood was visible, and the sun was nearing the horizon in the west. Taegan retrieved his bow and filled his quiver as they approached, and Zorvut followed suit.

"The giant boar here spend most of the day rooting around deeper in the forest, but we might find a straggler where the forest is less dense," he said, slowing his pace so Zorvut could catch up and he could speak more quietly. "Let's try and flush one out of the tree line first, if we can."

He nodded, and suggested, "I'll go left, you go right."

"Sure," Taegan agreed. "Stay within earshot, though."

They split up, and Taegan slowed Moonlight's pace to a leisurely trot, keeping a close eye on the underbrush. Giant boar were very large, but blended in easily with the drab browns and grays along the shaded forest floor, and could be hard to spot when not out in the open.

Taegan had gone nearly half a mile without spotting anything and was about to turn back when he felt a faint flash of surprise from the bond—they were quite far, so for him to feel it at all meant that it must have been a strong emotion, and he turned Moonlight around quickly. Faintly, he heard a shout, then the unmistakable squealing roar that meant Zorvut must have found a boar. He pressed his heels in harder to the horse's side and soon she was at a full gallop through the forest.

White-hot pain seared through his head, causing him to flinch and cry out involuntarily—he could hear a pained shout in the distance too, closer now but still too far to see. He winced, adrenaline pumping through him as if it were his own injury; but he could not tell where the wound was, only the pain from it.

"Taegan!" he heard Zorvut's voice call out.

"I'm coming!" he shouted in response, urging Moonlight to go faster although she was already at a full gallop. Finally, he could see the shape of Zorvut and Graksh't in the distance, and a giant boar darting around the horse's legs. He saw a flash of red, blood on its tusks—Zorvut had his bow out, but the boar was too close, and he was reaching for his sword on his back.

Taegan had drawn his bow and loosed an arrow before he could even think. The boar shrieked as the projectile pierced its side, whirling away from Zorvut. The beast was huge, large enough that it could surely topple Moonlight with one well-aimed lunge—the only reason it had not knocked Graksh't to the ground was because the horse was huge, too.

Its frantic eyes seemed to finally land on Taegan, and it reared up to charge; he drew his bow again, but Zorvut was already driving his sword down, just in time to catch it right near its hip. It screamed in agony and rage, pinned to the ground, unable to charge after either of them as Graksh't cantered away toward Taegan and Moonlight. The boar struggled only a moment longer before laying still, but Zorvut did not even stop to look at it as he rode up to Taegan and dismounted with obvious difficulty.

"Are you alright?" Taegan asked, breathless as he haphazardly looped his bow onto his back and leapt off his horse. Zorvut limped toward him before carefully lowering himself to the ground, and Taegan could see the injury on his calf. He dropped to his knees beside Zorvut, already yanking the stopper off his waterskin.

"I don't think it's bad," Zorvut said, pulling up his pant leg. "I didn't see it coming, is all."

"I shouldn't have left you," Taegan berated himself as he poured water over the wound. "I knew it was dangerous. We should have stayed together." Zorvut shook his head, but did not protest. Now that it was clean, it did not look as bad—the boar had slashed him, not gored him, so while it was still bleeding profusely, it was better than a deep wound that could fester. "I think I have a little bottle of alcohol and an extra shirt. I'll go get it."

He stood back up and hurried to Moonlight, digging through the saddlebag. He retrieved a small bottle of clear liquor, a cotton undershirt, and luckily found a tincture of willow bark, too—Aerik, thoughtful as he was, must have packed his bag. Turning back to face Zorvut, he caught the orc watching him intently. His heart was still pounding, and he could feel the adrenaline and pain radiating from the bond as well.

"This will help, too," he said, sitting back down next to him. "The alcohol first—ready?" Zorvut nodded, and Taegan poured it over the wound; he could see Zorvut clench his fists in the dirt, his eyes squeezing shut, but he made no sound. He realized he must have suppressed it from the bond, too, for he no longer felt the pinprick of pain at the base of his skull. "There. That's the worst of it. This should ease the pain." He soaked a corner of the cotton shirt with the tincture and pressed it to the wound. The white shirt was soon stained with red, but Zorvut visibly relaxed after a moment, and Taegan set to work wrapping the wound.

"Thank you," Zorvut said softly, his voice a low rumble in his chest. Taegan tied the makeshift bandage tightly, then glanced up to meet his gaze. When their eyes met, a thunderbolt of adrenaline-fueled arousal coursed through the bond. Taegan blinked in surprise, but he was instantly hard.

"Do you...?" he started to ask hesitantly.

"Yes," Zorvut replied before he could finish, his hands already unlacing Taegan's shirt. The primal, frenzied need coming from him was unlike anything Taegan had ever sensed from him before and soon he was caught up in it as well, letting Zorvut pull his clothes off while he frantically unbuttoned the orc's breeches. His cock was already rock-hard and straining against the cloth, springing free easily as soon as the buttons were undone.

Taegan started to climb into Zorvut's lap, but hesitated, eyeing the fresh bandage. "I don't want to hurt you," he said.

"You couldn't," Zorvut laughed, and pulled Taegan up to straddle him. His big hands spread Taegan's ass cheeks apart, rubbing his cock teasingly against the slick hole. Immediately all concern was gone from his mind, and he pressed back against him, feeling the head of his cock pushing him open. He moaned as he lowered himself onto it, but it became a keening cry as Zorvut immediately began to fuck him, shallow and teasing but still somehow overwhelming. His fingers were tangled in Zorvut's dark hair as he clung to his neck, pressing his face into the space between Zorvut's neck and shoulder.

"Gods," he whimpered, somehow already right on the edge of coming. Everything had happened so fast. "Fuck, Zorvut, *please*—" The orc growled in his ear, one hand enveloping his cock, stroking him rapidly in time with his thrusts. Taegan bit back a wail as he came, his body clenching hard around the massive cock inside him.

"So tight," Zorvut groaned, sending aftershocks of pleasure coursing through Taegan as he moved in long, slow, decadent thrusts. He gripped Taegan's hips, holding him in place and watching his cock disappear in and out of his body. Still, though, he was careful to only enter halfway—Taegan tried to push down, to take in more, but Zorvut held him firmly in place. Every single one of his nerves was on fire, heat radiating from the bond like a tiny sun. He could feel Zorvut about to come, and his own cock twitched eagerly, already desperate for more stimulation. He touched himself, biting his lip to stifle a moan.

"No, I want to hear you," Zorvut growled, pulling one of his hands away to pull Taegan's mouth open, his thumb pressing inside. Taegan moaned aloud, and felt the pleasure it elicited in Zorvut, and he was coming again, his cock pulsating with wave after wave of bliss.

"Please," he whimpered around Zorvut's fingers still in his mouth as he came. "Please come, please come inside me—" Zorvut's breathing hitched and he gave a few more hard thrusts, coming with a gasp. It filled him quickly, white-hot against his insides until his whole abdomen radiated with pleasure and warmth.

For a long moment he could only gasp and pant, trying to catch his breath, then moaned as Zorvut moved inside him. He pulled out gingerly, but a gush of liquid spilled out of Taegan, a slick mixture of come and his own lubrication. He sucked in a sharp breath, feeling his hole twitching at the sudden loss, still dripping with the overflow of fluid. A softer pleasure shivered down his spine, and he realized Zorvut's hand had moved to the back of his head and was idly stroking his hair—when he looked, the orc's eyes were still closed, his head tilted back in the blissful afterglow.

All his muscles felt suddenly weak, so he leaned forward, resting his head on Zorvut's shoulder. Zorvut wrapped his arms around him, pressing him closer to his chest. Taegan closed his eyes, letting himself get lost in the comforting sensation. He was not sure how long they remained there, but eventually he whispered against Zorvut's skin, "We should set up camp."

A faint laugh rumbled through Zorvut's chest. "We should," he agreed, and finally released Taegan from his embrace.

By the time the sun had fully set, they had a campfire set up and butchered the boar, with a haunch roasting over the flame. Graksh't and Moonlight were tethered to a tree, and Zorvut had set up their tent just beyond the treeline while Taegan tended to the fire. With the tent prepared, Zorvut sat down next to Taegan in front of the fire as they waited for the meat to finish roasting.

"Thank you," he said simply, and Taegan raised an eyebrow at him. "For helping me earlier. I... Well, to be honest, I'm embarrassed for not having seen the boar in the first place."

"Of course," Taegan said, surprised. "Of course I would help you."

"Still," he replied, looking visibly flustered as he glanced away. "Thank you."

"You're welcome," Taegan answered, suppressing a smile. He lifted the boar meat off the fire—it looked just about done.

They shared a quiet meal and watched the stars for a little while. Taegan thought about what he wanted to say and put his hand on Zorvut's knee.

"Since we are being honest with each other," he said slowly, keeping his gaze on his hand. "Can I... talk with you about something?" He could feel Zorvut hesitate, then nod.

"Of course," he replied, gesturing with an open palm for Taegan to continue.

"I don't think this will be surprising to you," he said, "But I had a lot of anger, at first, about not marrying another elf. This has been a hard adjustment—for both of us, I'm sure."

"I know," Zorvut said in acknowledgment, nodding.

"But," Taegan continued. "I do want to make this work, Zorvut. Not just for my father, and the peace treaty, but..." He could feel his face flush, and he squeezed his eyes shut. "For us. I don't want to be in a loveless marriage. I want us to get along, to... be fond of each other."

For a long moment, Zorvut did not respond. Whatever he was feeling was a strange mix of emotions through the bond. Finally, he gingerly placed his hand over Taegan's.

"Let me tell you something, too," he said. "I always thought my father offered me up just to have me sent away from the clan. I know I told you I never fit in, but... I have always been less than my siblings in his eyes, I think. We constantly competed for his attention, and..." He looked away, a flash of sadness coming through the bond. "I don't think I ever really felt like my family loved me. Well, my mother doted on me because I was small, but there was always a... a distance, between me and my siblings and my father. And the other members of our clan, they got along well with me, but maybe only because I was the warlord's son. I always had that thought. So I had no hope of finding a mate, and when he told me he would offer me for the peace treaty, I just... accepted it. I figured I would never find anyone regardless, that no other orc would want to be with me. And maybe I was right."

Underneath Zorvut's grasp, Taegan's hand clenched into a fist. His words were not surprising, but were still painful for him to hear spoken aloud. Part of him had known that Zorvut must not have fit in; he was quiet, thoughtful, and kind, the opposite of every orcish stereotype. But he had never considered why Zorvut would have agreed to be his father's offering—his own father had not had a choice, having only one child. Having to compete for his father's love certainly would have driven him to agree to an offer for something he did not even want.

"*I* want to be with you," he said, the forcefulness in his voice taking them both by surprise. "Zorvut, our marriage may have been only a symbol of peace at first, but what I feel for you is genuine. I accept you just as you are, and I... I hope we can have a real relationship with each other. I want that for us."

When he looked back up at Zorvut, there was a tenderness in his face that Taegan could not recall having ever seen before, and something like hope glimmered in the bond.

"I want that, too," Zorvut replied.

"The other day, when I was frustrated," Taegan offered. "The man we met in the library, he's... We had had a previous relationship. Shortly before we were married." He glanced away, feeling suddenly embarrassed. "I was angry he had approached me in front of you. I had asked him to leave me alone, and he wouldn't." He could feel anger and something like protectiveness stirring from Zorvut, and he quickly raised his free hand in a placating gesture. "It wasn't like that, though, and I don't think he'll bother me again. I gave him a rather stern talking-to, and that's why I was still upset when I came back. I wasn't mad at you, truly, and I'm sorry for how I reacted. And I thought you should know, if we want to have a real relationship with each other."

Zorvut nodded, seeming appeased. "I understand. And if he still doesn't leave you alone, well..." He made a slashing motion with his hand, the way Taegan had earlier, and the elf laughed in spite of himself.

"Did you have anyone like that?" he asked, and Zorvut grimaced.

"I did," he said. "It was purely physical, really, but... I thought I would say goodbye to him, the night of the procession, but he was... colder than I expected. Truth be told, I think he just wanted a way to get in good graces with my father." He let out a bitter laugh at that, and Taegan nodded knowingly.

"I think that might have been the case for me, too," he sighed, and smiled. "I suppose that's one decent thing to come out of all this. No more suitors who only care for the title we come with." He leaned into Zorvut's shoulder, and the orc's other arm came up to embrace him again.

After a moment, Zorvut pulled away to look Taegan in the face, who looked up at him questioningly. "Can I..." he started, color rising in his face—when he blushed, his gray-green skin took on a darker, more grayish tone. "I want to kiss you."

The spike of fear that flashed through the bond as he said it gave Taegan a hot moment of pain, remembering with regret the times he had turned aside before. Despite the heat he felt prickling up his own face, he nodded.

Zorvut's hand came up to cup his face, and he instinctively reached up to clasp it, his hand curling around the orc's forefinger as he drew his face up, closer to him. This time Taegan did not turn away, closing his eyes.

There was a faint flash of fear as he felt the hard, unyielding tusks brush against the side of his mouth, but Zorvut tilted his head and their lips fit together perfectly. The kiss was chaste and brief, but somehow Taegan still felt dizzy when he pulled away. He opened his eyes to see Zorvut watching him closely, his golden-yellow eyes gleaming in the light of the moon, and Taegan leaned in to kiss him again. This time, he let his mouth open against Zorvut's, a soft noise escaping his throat as their tongues met.

"My husband," he breathed when they finally parted. He felt Zorvut groan, a low rumble deep in his chest, desire burning through him at the word.

"I want you again," he said, pulling Taegan closer to him, and already he was nodding in agreement, pushing Zorvut's shirt up. They undressed quickly, and Zorvut laid him down on their blanket, leaning back to look at him.

"My husband," Zorvut echoed in a low growl, and Taegan smiled, stretching ostentatiously so the flickering light of the fire reflected off his skin like a multitude of tiny stars. Zorvut admired him for only a moment longer before lowering his body over Taegan's and trailing kisses along his throat and collarbones. "My husband..."

"Yours," Taegan agreed breathlessly, running his hands along the rippling muscles of Zorvut's back. He gasped as the orc's fingers found his hole, wet and pliant, and slid in effortlessly. "W-Wait," he stammered, and Zorvut froze, meeting his gaze questioningly. "No more holding back. I want to feel you, all of you."

Zorvut looked away, visibly hesitating. "I don't want to hurt you," he said softly, and Taegan shook his head.

"You couldn't," he said, then laughed. "Well, you could, but I'll tell you if you do. I promise. Please trust me." He hesitated a moment longer, still seeming unconvinced, then nodded.

"Alright," he agreed, and moved his fingers inside Taegan again. "Touch yourself. It would be easier if you come first."

That would be easy, Taegan thought with a grin. Obediently, he lowered a hand to stroke his cock, and Zorvut leaned back again to watch him while still working him open with his fingers. While it was nowhere near as satisfyingly full as his cock, the gentle movement inside him along with the stimulation of his own cock made quick work of him, and it did not take long before he was shooting come onto his belly with a shuddering gasp, Zorvut's fingers stretching him open even as he clenched around them.

Zorvut's fingers left him after that, pushing his legs up and around his waist. The orc kissed him again roughly, and Taegan moaned into his mouth as he felt his cock driving into him, the familiar fullness sending a shockwave of bliss through his body. At first Zorvut carefully only entered him halfway, moving in gentle, slow strokes.

"Come on," Taegan panted, breaking their kiss. Zorvut nodded, wordlessly leaning back. Gingerly, slowly, he pushed himself further into Taegan. He could feel his cock stretching him open further, deeper than he had ever been touched before—he groaned in half-pleasure, half-pain, his head falling back and his hands clutching desperately at the blanket underneath him.

Zorvut kept pushing in, and in, and just when Taegan was sure he was going to break apart and nearly cried out for him to stop, he felt Zorvut's hard abs against his thighs as the orc let out a sigh of pleasure. He had done it.

"Fuck," he panted, his eyes fluttering open. "Oh, *fuck*." Looking down, he could *see* his belly bulging with Zorvut's cock. He gingerly ran his fingers along his stomach, pressing into the foreign firmness underneath. "Look, look—gods, you're so *big*." Zorvut nodded silently, his eyes trained on the bulge he had created, desire burning fiery hot from the bond.

The sensation was unlike anything Taegan had ever felt before. The fullness of it was the only feeling he could focus on; every cell in his body was alight with the fear that he was about to be torn in two yet simultaneously begging for more.

Then Zorvut began to fuck him, and he screamed out, his cock spurting weakly as the orgasm shattered through his overstimulated nerves.

"Yes," he wailed as Zorvut fucked him through it. "Gods, yes, please don't stop—ah—fuck—ah—*ah!*" His cries devolved into wordless sounds as he buried his face in Zorvut's shoulder—faintly he could feel the orc kissing him, his neck and face and shoulders, murmuring something he couldn't understand. His sole focus had become the unbearable fullness thrusting impossibly deep inside him, drowning out every other sensation.

"Mine," he could just make out Zorvut's growl as the rhythmic thrusting stuttered and stopped. "You're mine. You're mine."

Taegan could feel the hot liquid pouring through the deepest parts of his insides, filling him impossibly tighter, as Zorvut came inside him. The sheer pleasure cycling between them through their bond was enough to make his own cock twitch despite being utterly spent.

Finally, as the waves of bliss seemed to eventually recede, Zorvut took in a deep, steadying breath and began to pull away.

"Oh, gods," Taegan moaned; it felt as if his cock went on for miles as it slipped out of him, glistening and dripping with his slick. "Ah—fuck!" The burning stretch ended abruptly as Zorvut fully left him, but he could feel his hole gaping desperately at the sudden emptiness, and he watched as a thick, steady stream of come gushed out of him. Zorvut stared in aroused fascination as the viscous fluid poured out of him—the intensity of his gaze as Taegan was splayed out in such a vulnerable position made his cock twitch in interest, though he was sure he could not come again even if he tried.

"You're incredible," Zorvut finally murmured as they caught their breath, and Taegan laughed. "No, really. I didn't think.... I didn't think that was possible."

"Well, if you had any doubt of it before, I think you've well and truly ruined me now," Taegan replied, propping himself up on his elbows. He had no idea how to even begin cleaning himself off. "I *am* yours."

A small smile played at Zorvut's lips and he leaned in to gently kiss Taegan again. "My husband," he murmured. "My husband."

# Chapter Nine

They set back out the following morning, their prize in tow. Zorvut trotted alongside Taegan this time, although Graksh't had such a longer stride than Moonlight that he occasionally had to pause for the smaller horse to catch up. But their pace was leisurely, and their conversation was not nearly as uncomfortable or as strained as the meager words they had shared during yesterday's trip. Mostly, Taegan asked him all kinds of questions about himself—he wanted to know everything he could about Zorvut. Since the orc had come to live in the elven capital, he felt that Zorvut knew more about him than he knew about Zorvut, but he intended to soon close the gap between them.

Zorvut had always preferred other men. His favorite sibling was one of his younger sisters, Gorza. He was more like his mother than his father. His first kill had been a rabbit when he was seven. He was fourteen when he had been in his first real skirmish on the battlefield. Though he favored his greatsword, he could handle just about any weapon, but he didn't like polearms or javelins. He spoke four languages; orcish, elvish, and two human dialects. Books were scarce in a clan of nomads, but he always read any tome that made its way into his hands.

"What's your favorite color?" Taegan asked when he had finally worked through all the questions he had brainstormed about Zorvut's childhood and history. The orc chuckled, shaking his head.

"Favorite color?" he repeated. "I don't know. Red? What's yours?"

"Purple," Taegan answered after a moment of consideration, but before he could think of another question, Zorvut said quickly,

"I want to ask you something first."

"Go on, then," Taegan replied, his eyebrows raising in surprise.

"Well," Zorvut said slowly, suddenly seeming to reconsider. "I guess I don't understand exactly how, ah, reproduction works for you. There are rumors and stereotypes about elves, but I wouldn't trust any of that to be the truth."

At that, Taegan laughed. "You've been thinking of reproduction more often, I suppose," he teased, but the flustered expression on Zorvut's face remained serious. "It is a little different, but not that much. It was said that in ancient times, elves were all one sex, but have evolved over time to have two, like other humanoid races. I'm not sure how true that is either, but it is definitely true that elves can have biological children with any combination of the sexes."

"So, right now, you could..." Zorvut said, trailing off uncertainly. He trained his eyes on Taegan's belly, and he shook his head quickly with a start of realization.

"No, no," he stammered, glancing away. He was not sure why he felt suddenly embarrassed. "There is some difference. For males, it's more like a heat—it only occurs once or twice a year, rather than monthly, but it, ah, lasts a bit longer, as well."

"I see," Zorvut said, though there was still discernible confusion stemming from his end of the bond. "And would two males always have male children?"

"No, it could still be either," he said, then paused. "Although I'm less sure about two different races. I know with two elves, we're similar enough genetically that any combination could produce either sex. I don't know if that would remain the same for us. Or, of course, any other half-elf."

"Of course," Zorvut said, nodding, then glanced away. "Could I ask, was it the king who...?"

"No, my other father," Taegan said, shaking his head with a slight smile. "Father always said I looked more like Papa since he was the one who carried me."

Zorvut nodded wordlessly, still mulling over the information. His expression was hard to read, but from the bond, it felt like he was deep in thought.

"Is there a lot of pressure for you to produce an heir? Soon?" he finally asked, not quite meeting Taegan's gaze. He pursed his lips, considering the question.

"Well, no," he said slowly. "I mean, since Papa died before they had more children, I've known that the royal bloodline would carry on through me, so it's always been sort of a given, I suppose. But I am still young enough that most think of me as the current heir, so no need for a *new* heir yet. My father didn't become king until he was nearly a hundred, I think. I'm sure it would be very different if I were already king, though."

"Makes sense," Zorvut agreed. "For me... For orcs in general, since so many are slain in battle, there is a lot of pressure to have children young, and as many as you can. Not that I have any, though!" He waved his hand in a suddenly startled motion, and Taegan chuckled. "I suppose what I'm trying to get at is, do you... *want* children? With me?"

The seriousness in his tone made Taegan pause. His uncertainty was understandable, but even if Zorvut had asked the same question before their heart-to-heart last night, Taegan's sense of duty would have driven him to the same answer.

"Yes," he said firmly, nodding. "I mean, maybe not for a while yet. But... well, when I think of having children, I think of the joy I shared with my fathers when I was a child. I think my childhood was a very happy one because of my fathers and their love for me, and the thought of being able to give that same happiness to another..." He trailed off, the sentiment feeling silly even to his own ears. But he could feel a warmth coming from Zorvut, and he glanced over to see a soft, almost tender expression on his face.

"I think that's admirable," Zorvut replied, and Taegan smiled, glancing away again in embarrassment. "I... Well, I do worry, though. I worry that a half-orc's life will always be needlessly difficult, even for a prince. Or princess. I know well enough how it is to not be accepted, and I can imagine how much worse it could be for a half breed, for someone who truly doesn't fit in anywhere."

Taegan frowned at that. There was certainly some truth to what he was saying, and it was a valid concern. He had considered his children would be half-elves, but they would also be half-orcs. Neither had ever been a ruling monarch of the kingdom, so they had already ensured their children would be the first of their kind. And while there could be a particular freedom in setting that precedent, there would be just as much pressure, if not more.

"That's fair," Taegan replied slowly. "But let me assure you of this. The stereotype of elves is that we are all the same, but the truth is that as a culture we've committed to working together despite our differences. The elves of Aefraya have always remained loyal to the monarchy, because we trust that the gods have provided our monarchs with the wisdom to rule well. So some might put up a fuss, but when it comes down to it, I have no doubt that they will fall in line behind whoever ascends the throne. Including us, and our descendants."

Zorvut did not seem entirely convinced, but the words comforted him and he nodded.

"I trust your judgment," he said. "That was all I wanted to ask. Continue."

"In that case," Taegan said with a laugh. "Hmm. What's your favorite food?"

They arrived back at the castle a bit after midday, and the butchered boar was carted off to the kitchens, where it would make a fine roast for the evening meal. One servant took Moonlight's reins to return her to the stable.

"I'll go put Graksh't away," Zorvut said before Taegan could turn to leave. "He's been skittish the last few times the servants have handled him. I don't think he trusts them yet."

"You should go have your leg looked at, too. Just in case," Taegan replied. Zorvut seemed to hesitate for a moment, then reached for Taegan's hand, lifting it to his lips to kiss softly. Heat instantly flooded his face with the sudden display of affection.

"I'll meet you for dinner," Zorvut said simply, and turned to go.

"Y-yes," Taegan stammered in agreement—though there were only a few elves around, he could feel their curious gazes on him.

"My prince," a voice came behind him, and he turned to find Aerik, looking as politely disinterested as ever. "The king requests your presence in the throne room."

"Of course," he replied brusquely, pushing the tingling sensation lingering in his hand out of his mind. "Tell him I'll be there shortly. I'm just going to put on some clean clothes."

He found a fresh outfit had already been laid out for him when he returned to their quarters, and he made a mental note to ask Aerik to draw him a bath as well—even with a clean change of clothes, he could still smell horse and sweat on him. Whatever his father wanted, he hoped it would be quick.

The doors to the throne room were closed, but not guarded, so when Taegan arrived, he pushed them open gingerly to peek in before entering.

"Ah, Taegan," the king's voice called out the moment he looked in. "Good, I heard you were back. Come in, come in."

When he entered, his father was seated on the throne, and a handful of nobles stood before him. Taegan recognized them, all local barons and landowners—they bowed their heads respectfully at him as he stepped toward them, and he nodded in acknowledgment.

"You needed me?" he asked as he approached the throne, lowering his head as he addressed his father.

"Not immediately, though I did want to ask you to join me for a few meetings I have tomorrow. The council of landowners will meet again tomorrow morning to settle some border disputes and discuss the expected harvest. I thought it would be good for you to listen in." King Ruven smiled wryly. "And I just wanted to know how my son's hunting trip went."

"Excellently," Taegan replied, suppressing a smile of his own. "We slew a giant boar, mostly unscathed. The kitchen should be preparing it for tonight."

"Mostly?" Ruven repeated, raising an eyebrow. "Are you both alright?"

"Yes, but Zorvut had a minor injury. I believe he's having it looked over now, though I don't think it's serious. The beast grazed his leg."

"Lucky, then—being gored by a giant boar is a much more serious matter. Forgive me, my lords—" He turned to address the nobles who had been waiting in polite silence. "Give me just a moment longer and we can return to our discussion. Taegan, I can expect to see you both at dinner, then?"

"Yes, of course," he replied, then hesitated before adding, "Father, if you want me to join your talks tomorrow, perhaps Zorvut should join as well. I'd like to have him get more involved in the goings-on of the castle, and he is eager to learn."

The group of barons all swiveled their heads to look at him as if on cue—though their expressions betrayed little, they were still clearly startled by the request. King Ruven seemed surprised as well, though it was a more mild reaction, as if the thought had not even occurred to him.

"Of course," he replied after a beat of silence. "I think that would be an excellent idea." One of the barons shifted uncomfortably, but none said anything, and King Ruven seemed not to notice—if he did, he did not acknowledge it.

"Thank you," Taegan replied, bowing his head and hoping the smugness he felt was not apparent on his face. "I will let him know, and we will see you at dinner. If I may take my leave?"

"Go on, then," the king replied with a lazy wave of his hand, and his attention returned to the nobles he had been speaking with.

Taegan left the room quietly to make his way back to their quarters. This time when he opened the door, Zorvut was inside, and he could hear the telltale splash of the bath being drawn.

"I thought we could both use a bath," Zorvut said as Taegan entered, smiling.

"An excellent plan," Taegan agreed. "I have some news. We're both to be present in some meetings and talks with the local council of landowners tomorrow morning. Dry conversation, but good to know."

"Both of us?" Zorvut repeated, surprised. Taegan nodded, stifling a chuckle.

"Trying to get out of it already?" he asked. "Yes, both of us. I thought it would be proper for you to be included. I already know a lot of the boring stuff, but if we're both to rule someday, you should learn, too."

"True," Zorvut replied, but furrowed his nose begrudgingly. "I will join, then."

"Good," Taegan said, and stepped closer to him, leaning into his chest. "And is your leg alright?"

"Should be fine as long as I keep it clean," he said—when they were this close, his voice sounded like a distant rumble of thunder in his chest. One of his arms raised to hold Taegan more tightly against him. "Forgive me if I was too bold earlier."

"There is nothing to forgive," Taegan said quickly, looking up at him with a smirk. "In fact, as your princely duty, I expect you to kiss my hand every time we must part."

"Is that so? And what about for me?"

"You get the pleasure of kissing my hand, of course," he teased.

"And if I want to kiss you here?" His thumb brushed over Taegan's lips, sending a shiver down his spine. "Or here?" It trailed down his neck and traced his collarbone.

"Well," Taegan replied slowly, suddenly feeling very distracted. "You *are* my prince, so you could kiss wherever you want. I won't protest."

Zorvut opened his mouth to reply, but was abruptly interrupted. "Forgive the intrusion, my prince," Aerik's voice came from the bathroom, making Taegan's heart leap up into his throat. "But the bath is ready for you now. I'll leave you to it." He could hear the stone door of the servant exit swing open and shut, then Taegan let out a laugh of embarrassment.

"Gods, I forgot he was here," he said, covering his face and stepping away from Zorvut, who released him with a chuckle. "Come along, then. I don't want to smell like a horse for a moment longer."

# Chapter Ten

Over the course of the next several days, Taegan made it a point to be more openly affectionate with his husband. If any of the elves in the castle were still secretly uncomfortable with Zorvut's presence, he figured, he would *make* them get used to him. He held Zorvut's hand nearly everywhere that they went together, kissed him when they parted, embraced him when they rejoined. They often sat together in the library reading, rather than taking books back to his study to read in private—though he did enjoy reading aloud to Zorvut when they were indeed alone.

At first, he felt more self-conscious than he could ever remember feeling in his life, and he could feel a similar discomfort through the bond from Zorvut. Forcing himself to reveal the softer, kinder feelings he had toward Zorvut was a struggle after trying to hide them for so long. But it was important, he explained over breakfast the next morning, because the more often they presented themselves as a unified front to the world, the more naturally it would come to them over time.

Their bond was something he made a point of learning more about, as well. He read the elven history of the marriage bond to Zorvut, remarking with a tinge of bitterness that he had never really explained the way elven bonds of marriage worked.

"The strength of the bond can vary, although the reasons behind it are not fully understood," Taegan said as he leaned forward over the book he was reading. "I wasn't sure at first, but I think we seem to have an unusually strong bond, especially for a bond between races. Even my father mentioned the bond between him and my Papa was not very strong at first."

"Is it just compatibility?" Zorvut asked. He was lounging in one of the large, comfy chairs in the study while Taegan sat at his desk.

"No," Taegan said, shaking his head. "Well, I don't think so. I would suspect it has something to do with the latent magical ability of one or both, but I don't have much affinity for magic. Do you?"

"Orcs typically don't have magic either," Zorvut answered with a laugh. "I've never tried, but I doubt I could do anything at all. What can you do? I've never seen you use magic, now that you mention it."

"I can't do much," he admitted, glancing away. Though he had been reassured over and over again that magical ability was innate and there was no shame in his meager ability, a lingering embarrassment still squeezed at his chest whenever he spoke of it. "When I was a child, I had always hoped I could become a powerful warlock one day, but it just isn't in my blood. My father, the king, is a decent mage, but his skill is rather average. Papa couldn't do much magic either, and I turned out more like him. Most elves can do at least a bit of simple magic, though. Let me try..."

He turned his focus to a candle on the opposite end of his desk, holding a hand toward it. Unblinking, he watched the flickering of the flame, trying to grasp at the glimmer of *something* in his chest that he always felt when trying to use whatever small spark of magic he had. It was a hard feeling to describe—like walking in a dream behind someone he could not see yet somehow still knew was there. He focused on the unnameable feeling, tilted his hand to the right to make the flame lean in the same direction, then he clenched his fist with a flourish, and the candle snuffed out.

"Impressive," Zorvut said, giving a nod of approval.

"It's very little by elven standards," Taegan laughed, shaking his head.

"Far more than I could do," he insisted, then grinned. "Although it might have been faster just to blow out the candle." Taegan laughed at that.

"Well, I never claimed it was more efficient," he admitted with a shrug.

"Tell me more about the bond, then," Zorvut said. A soft fondness was welling up from his end of the bond; Taegan thought he just liked to hear him speak, and that made him smile.

"What else? Well, there is a limit to how far across the magic can connect," he continued, trying to think of what he had not already said. "It's not exact, and again can vary between couples, but usually about a mile is the very furthest it can connect." Zorvut blinked, seeming to think it over.

"Strange to think we've never been more than a mile apart since the day we met," he murmured, and Taegan nodded. "So what happens when we *are* a mile apart, then?"

"I'm not sure. Hopefully, we will not have to find out," Taegan replied, shrugging. A more somber mood seemed to overtake Zorvut suddenly, and he glanced up at him, raising a quizzical eyebrow.

"I was just thinking, orc lifespans are so much shorter than elves," Zorvut said slowly, not meeting Taegan's gaze. "I may live to a hundred at the very most, but you'll barely be middle-aged then. You may even still be a prince. When I die, what will happen to the bond?"

Taegan blinked, surprised at the turn the conversation had taken. "I don't know," he stammered, then took a moment to gather his thoughts before continuing. "When my father died, the king knew the instant it happened, even though they were far apart. So it must be different from just being separated by distance." He had a flash of a memory of that day—the image of his father's face suddenly going pale and still while he sat on his throne, the words he had been speaking trailing off before he turned away and vomited blood, bright crimson splattering against the white marble tile, was still perfectly clear in his mind even after all this time. With a shake of his head, he forced himself to focus on the conversation at hand, pushing the unpleasant memory away. "I'm sure there is some pain, though, obviously, it is survivable. I... don't think I've ever asked him about it in depth. I don't think I could."

"Understandable," Zorvut murmured, then finally met Taegan's gaze. "Sorry. I just had the thought, and... well, it seemed important to know. My apologies if that was too dark."

"No, no," Taegan said, shaking his head as if trying to shake off the lingering discomfort the question had left him with. "It's good to have these kinds of conversations. It's something I had never really considered before, but... you're right." He pursed his lips. "That makes me sad to think about."

Zorvut shrugged. "That's always the case, though," he replied. "One will always die before the other. Well, maybe not always, but nearly always. No need to be afraid of it yet, though."

"Let's talk about something else for now, then," Taegan said. "There will be plenty of time for that sort of thing later. Do you still want to finish this book?" Zorvut looked at him with a wry smile, but nodded, and Taegan resumed reading.

It took only a few days to settle into their new normal. Just as Taegan had said, the more often they simply held hands or embraced throughout the castle, the easier it became—and the more it made Taegan's heart bubble over with affection, though he wasn't quite sure if he was comfortable enough to say so just yet.

They were walking together toward the archery range late in the morning when the king's voice came from behind them.

"Taegan!" King Ruven called, and they both turned quickly to face him. Taegan bowed his head slightly, and Zorvut followed suit. "I'm glad I found you. Could I have a quick word, in private?" The king smiled at the surreptitious glance that Taegan and Zorvut shared.

"Nothing bad, I assure you. I just wanted to speak with you, my son."

"Of course," Taegan agreed, then glanced at Zorvut. "Don't wait up, I'll meet you out there."

"I'll have your things set up," Zorvut agreed, and released Taegan's hand. He tilted his head up expectantly, but Zorvut hesitated, then instead pulled Taegan's hand up to his lips before giving another polite bow of his head to the king and continuing on his way.

"Is anything the matter?" Taegan asked as he joined his father, who started walking leisurely back the way they had come.

"No, not at all," he said, a slight smile on his lips. "It's just strange not to have all your time to myself anymore."

Taegan chuckled. "I hate to be the one to say it, but it *was* your idea," he replied, and the king laughed aloud at that.

"I'm glad to see you've been in a good mood," he said, then gave a more knowing glance to Taegan. "Both of you seem to be getting along better as of late."

"Yes," Taegan agreed, glancing away. Already he could feel his face flush with embarrassment. "Your advice definitely helped me. It took a few conversations, but we are getting along much better than I would have anticipated."

"Good," Ruven said. They were walking in the general direction of the king's private quarters, but with much less purpose than Taegan was used to seeing from his father. "I appreciate how much Zorvut also seems to want things to be successful, both between our nations and the two of you directly. I don't know if he is yet comfortable enough around me for it to mean anything if I said that to him, but perhaps you can pass my thanks along to him."

"Of course," Taegan said, nodding. The king's expression tensed, as if he wanted to say more, so he waited, but Ruven seemed to be weighing his words.

"Taegan," he finally said, looking into the distance. "Do you think you'll be able to be happy this way? Maybe not now, but someday?"

The question took Taegan by surprise, and he almost missed a step as they walked, catching himself before he could stumble.

"Yes," he said, nodding even as he glanced away, his face reddening. "Zorvut and I have been getting along very well. I enjoy his company, and..."

He paused, unsure if he could admit it. "And I think... I think I may love him."

The king turned to look at him as he said it, his eyebrows raised but his expression otherwise unreadable. "And does he feel the same?" he asked, his voice much softer than Taegan would have expected.

"I think so," he answered. "I don't know. I haven't said it yet. But I hope he feels the same. I think he does." He was stammering now, and he shut his mouth firmly before he could say anything more embarrassing. When he glanced back over at Ruven, a soft smile was playing at his lips, though he was clearly still trying to maintain the same stoic expression as always.

"Well," he replied slowly. "That is surprising to me, but a pleasant surprise. Taegan, I know all this must have felt like a sacrifice to you, and in many ways it has been. But it has always been my hope that you can still find happiness, and if he brings you happiness, then I will be happy as well. You are my only son, and I love you more than anything in this world."

"Father," Taegan protested, feeling his face burning red. Luckily, no one was around to witness the vulnerable conversation. "I know."

"It's the truth," the king said, and he squeezed Taegan's shoulder affectionately. "But I will stop embarrassing you for today. Go on, then. Can I expect you both at dinner?"

"Yes, we'll see you then," Taegan said with a nod, and he bowed his head to go.

When he arrived back at the archery range, Zorvut was standing a little way into the range with their equipment. Closer to the castle, two children were practicing with shortbows, aiming at some of the large straw targets closest to the storage shed. Taegan recognized them as children of one of the castle knights, a brother and sister. Noticing him, they gave quick bows of their heads, which Taegan returned as he walked by.

Behind him, he heard a wooden *thunk* as one of their arrows was loosed, then a childish squeal.

"Too high!" he heard the girl exclaim. "Ezran! You shot it too high, and now I can't reach."

Taegan turned to look, but Zorvut was already approaching. The arrow was at an awkward angle at the very top of the target, as if the arrow had sailed upward then pierced the target on its way back down. The girl had run up to the target, but both children glanced over at the sound of their approach. A hesitant expression came over the girl's face, the smaller boy openly scowling.

"Here," Zorvut said, effortlessly pulling the arrow from the target. He leaned down to extend it to the girl, who took it nervously, glancing between him and Taegan before stepping away, closer to her younger brother.

"You're the orc," the boy said bluntly, and his sister visibly cringed, shushing him. Taegan frowned and stepped forward, but Zorvut raised a reassuring hand.

"I am," he said to the boy. "And you're an elf. And I've just helped you get your arrow back." The boy frowned, glancing away with a chagrined expression.

"Thank you," he mumbled.

"Thank you," the girl repeated, a little more confidently. With that, Zorvut turned and rejoined Taegan.

"That was kind of you," Taegan said quietly as they walked. Zorvut shrugged and replied,

"Maybe it will help them be a little less scared next time they see me."

That was how most of their days went for the next few weeks. Taegan and Zorvut were rarely apart, but Taegan found that the more time they spent together, the more joy it brought him. He had not expected to find such happiness in spending lazy afternoons reading together or simply lounging in the gardens under the sun, but the quiet moments between them became some of the most imprinted in his memory. He could not quite bring himself to speak his feelings aloud, but he knew that Zorvut could feel the soft, warm affection that welled up in him from the other end of the bond. That was enough, he hoped, at least for now.

Everything was going better than he could have imagined, until they were awoken in the middle of the night to the sound of someone pounding on their door.

The sudden noise echoed sharply through their chambers, Zorvut immediately leaping up from their bed out of instinct, Taegan more groggily stumbling to his feet. He could feel Zorvut was just as startled as he was, adrenaline coursing between them.

"Who could it possibly be?" he muttered as Zorvut cautiously approached the door. Their eyes met, and Zorvut slowly reached for a knife on the table—not even a knife, a letter-opener—and held it behind his back as he reached for the door handle. Taegan nodded anxiously, remaining where he was.

In one quick movement, Zorvut twisted the door handle and pulled it open, revealing the form of Kelvhan, illuminated by the light of a single candle which he held in his hands. Zorvut's face twisted into a scowl at the sight of him, and Taegan took a startled step back.

"What are you doing here?" he blurted before either could speak—now that he could get a good look at the other elf, Kelvhan's expression seemed hurried, almost afraid. He tried to step into the room, but Zorvut held out a hand, stopping him.

"He asked you a question," he snarled, his lips curled around his tusks in a fearsome display Taegan had never seen on his face before.

"Please, may I come in?" Kelvhan asked breathlessly, as if he had just run up the stairs to their quarters. He very well may have run, Taegan thought as he looked him over. Zorvut glanced over at Taegan for permission, but he hesitated.

"Why?" he pressed, shaking his head. "Why are you here?"

"Please! It's important!" Kelvhan begged, looking wildly between them before lowering his voice to a harsh whisper. "I'm here to warn you. Your very lives are in danger."

# Chapter Eleven

A stunned silence fell over the room for a brief moment as Taegan glanced uneasily between the two figures standing at the door. Finally, he managed to gesture for Kelvhan to enter, and Zorvut let him in, closing the door behind him.

"What do you mean, we're in danger?" Taegan pressed as Kelvhan entered the chamber, setting the candle down. He could see the warlock's hands were shaking. "What's happened?"

"Last week, I had a vision," Kelvhan said, quiet but urgent. Zorvut watched him intently, still standing in the doorway, like a hunter tracking its prey—even if he hadn't felt suspicion radiating from the bond, Taegan could tell Zorvut didn't trust him at all. "A... sense that something wasn't right. Taegan, you know my magic, you know I have some talent in divination. Right?"

"Yes, that's true," Taegan agreed slowly. "Where is this going?"

"I couldn't discern exactly what it was, but I knew where I had to go for answers. The orc homeland, the city of Drol Kuggradh," Kelvhan said. Taegan raised his eyebrows in surprise, as did Zorvut. "So I traveled there, and my divination led me to have a conversation with the wife of the warlord, Naydi. What she told me, I confirmed magically to be the truth." Zorvut's eyes had narrowed into a glare, even as Kelvhan turned to face him.

"Zorvut," he said, his voice low. "I hate to be the bearer of bad news. But you are not a son of Hrul Bonebreaker."

The cold, numbing shock that coursed through their bond made Taegan gasp, the only sound to break through the silence. He shook his head in disbelief, glancing between the two, but Zorvut's gaze was trained firmly on Kelvhan.

"Impossible," Zorvut said faintly, barely above a whisper. But Taegan could feel a faint, creeping dread starting to fracture his surprise, like a long-abandoned suspicion finally coming to light.

"I'm afraid it's true," Kelvhan said. "I can show you." With a flourish and a murmured incantation, an illusory form materialized above his outstretched hand—a face, slightly transparent, with a flickering, indistinct background that swirled and dissipated around it like mist. As the features came into focus, it was undoubtedly the warlord's wife Naydi, Zorvut's mother. Kelvhan truly must have gone to speak with her, Taegan realized, for he had not been at the wedding and otherwise never would have had the chance to see her.

The illusory face began to talk, the voice quiet and slightly distorted, but Zorvut still gave a start of recognition.

"*Zorvut is the runt of my children, yes,*" she said. "*- But he is only so because he is only half-orc. I could never admit such a thing to Hrul, but... Well, there was a traveling bard who came through our lands, by the name of Tomlin Whitmore. A very adventurous human, to be sure.*" She gave a humorless laugh, her eyes downcast. "*I suspected it, but I knew for certain when he was born—so small, and he never caught up with his siblings. But Hrul did not suspect, so I never said anything.*" Her expression became suddenly fearful, almost shocked, as if she had meant to say none of it. "*How did you—?!*"

Kelvhan gave another flourish of his wrist, and the image vanished. Zorvut's eyes were still locked on the spot where his mother's face had been, and Taegan could feel his shock sinking steadily into despair.

"You tricked her," Taegan found himself saying without thought. "You forced her to tell you. How can we know that any of that was true?"

"Taegan," Kelvhan said, shaking his head. "I... compelled her to speak with me, yes. But I cannot compel someone to lie. Everything she said was true."

Zorvut remained silent, finally looking away from them. He had to say something, Taegan thought, but what?

"Zorvut," he said, taking a step closer to his husband. "This changes nothing. You're still—"

"I'm afraid this changes everything," Kelvhan interrupted, grabbing Taegan by the forearm to stop him. Taegan wrenched his hand away with a scowl, but Kelvhan continued on. "If Zorvut is not a true-born heir of the warlord, then the terms of the peace treaty have not been met, and your union has been a deception. The moment Hrul Bonebreaker learned of his wife's indiscretion, he cast her away and rallied his armies. I returned as quickly as I could, but there's no telling how soon they'll be marching on us once again. And the news may very well be spreading even more rapidly. If the king finds out..."

"What?!" Taegan exclaimed. "For what purpose? If the warlord didn't know, if Zorvut himself didn't know, why then march on us now?" Kelvhan shrugged.

"I have no insight as to that, except that orcs are a bloodthirsty race," he said. "If there is no reason not to fight, then fight they shall."

Everything was happening so fast. Taegan stumbled back and sat weakly on the edge of the bed, his hands pressed to his face. Somehow his mind was racing yet completely blank at the same time—it felt as if everything precious had slipped out of his grasp, and he was trapped in its moment of free fall, watching helplessly before it shattered.

Kelvhan cleared his throat, and continued, "Zorvut, if you value your life at all, I would recommend that you flee. It is only a matter of time before King Ruven casts you out, or worse."

Zorvut had been silent, but finally looked up to meet Taegan's gaze—his golden-yellow eyes were glassy and wet. Taegan's heart squeezed in despair. He had never seen Zorvut cry before.

"Do you think that's true?" he asked in a low, urgent voice. From the bond, Taegan could finally put a name to the burning sensation he felt coming from Zorvut: fear.

"I—I don't know," Taegan stammered. Part of him balked at the thought of his father doing such a thing, yet King Ruven had worked so tirelessly on the peace treaty; he could not say with any certainty how he might react.

"Should I go?" he asked, stepping toward him. He knelt down and grasped Taegan's hands tightly, his own hands trembling. "Taegan, do you think he speaks the truth? Would it be safer for us if I left? Safer for you?"

In his mind, Taegan exclaimed that of course he did not want Zorvut to go, no matter what happened. But the words couldn't seem to form around his lips, and he could not push the image out of his mind of Zorvut being surrounded by castle guards, thrown into the dungeons beaten and bloody, or worse. Terror clenched in his throat as he tried to speak.

Zorvut's mouth tightened into a hard line at his silence. A spark of despair bloomed in the bond, and then was suddenly cut off—Taegan winced at the sudden emptiness, looking up in shock. Zorvut released his hands, moving methodically to pull his cloak from where it hung on the wall.

He must have closed his end of the bond, Taegan realized in a panic, as the back of his head felt suddenly raw and tender, as if a piece of his own mind had been neatly sliced away.

"Wait," he managed to gasp out, reaching his hands out uselessly. He could not bring himself to stand; every muscle in his body felt weak. "Zorvut, please."

"No, I understand," Zorvut said quietly, not meeting his gaze. "I want you to be safe. Taegan, I..." He looked to Taegan, his eyes burning with emotion that he could not identify, seemingly just as unable to form the words he wanted to say as Taegan was. "I'm sorry."

Zorvut fastened his cloak, opened the door, and was gone. Finally, Taegan managed to will himself to stand, stumbling after him, but Kelvhan stepped between him and the closed door.

"Wait!" he cried out, panic filling his voice. He could not seem to push past Kelvhan, his whole body trembling. "No, wait! Please! Zorvut!"

"Let him go," Kelvhan said, his voice a quiet whisper in Taegan's ear. "You have to let him go."

Taegan was not sure how long he stood there gasping for breath, staring desperately at the closed door and willing it to open again, willing Zorvut to return. But the door remained closed, and eventually Kelvhan gently pulled him away.

"We should go," he was saying as Taegan allowed himself to be moved, so dazed he barely processed the words. "The sooner we can alert the king, the better prepared we will be if the orcs try to launch an attack."

He nodded weakly and stumbled after Kelvhan. He could focus on nothing but the sudden, painful emptiness in his head—had this been what Zorvut had meant, the one time he had closed off the bond, when he said it was *uncomfortable*? There was certainly discomfort, but it seemed a tame word to describe the absence where there had just been a presence, like a tooth had been yanked out of his jaw and his tongue could not pull away from the tender, bleeding chasm where it once was. Before he realized it, they were ascending the spiral staircase to the king's chambers, and Taegan felt tears streaming silently down his face. He hastily wiped them away with his sleeve.

"Halt!" a voice exclaimed as they reached the top of the stairs. "Identify yourself!"

"It's me," Taegan said before Kelvhan could answer. "Please, I must see my father."

"Prince Taegan?" the guard stammered, immediately sheathing his weapon—Taegan had not realized it was drawn. "Forgive me, my prince. Are you—I mean, yes, I will get the king. Wait here."

The guard turned and opened the door, stepping carefully inside. Taegan could hear his voice saying quietly, "Forgive my intrusion, King Ruven, but the prince is asking for you. He's just outside." He heard a faint murmur in response, too quiet to make out. A moment later, the guard reappeared in the doorway, gesturing for them to enter.

As they stepped toward the door, Taegan felt Kelvhan's hand on his back—whether it was meant to be reassuring or guiding, he did not know, but he quickened his pace to pull away. The other elf seemed to take the hint, at least, and did not try to touch him again.

When they entered, King Ruven was standing and pulling a robe over his shoulders, blinking in the sudden light. The moment Taegan saw him, he could feel tears burning against his eyes again.

"Taegan?" he asked, the worry evident in his voice. "What's happened? And... Kelvhan, right? From the library? What's going on?"

"Please forgive the unusual intrusion, my king," Kelvhan said quickly, bowing his head deeply. "I would not ask for an audience if it were not of the utmost importance."

"Father," Taegan interrupted, his voice tremulous. "Kelvhan discovered that Zorvut is not the son of the warlord."

The king's expression remained blank for a long moment, then his brows furrowed in confusion. "What?" he asked, bewildered. "Where is he?"

"He fled," Taegan replied, and could not stop the sob that escaped him as he said it. He pressed a hand to his eyes. "I—I don't know where he is."

"Let me explain," Kelvhan offered, glancing between the two of them. "I am a practitioner of divination, my king, and recently I had a premonition that something was amiss. My inquiries led me to the orc homeland, where I was able to procure an audience with the wife of the warlord, Zorvut's mother, and she confirmed that he was, in fact, a half-orc, and not a son of Hrul Bonebreaker."

King Ruven's expression had slowly morphed from shock to a grim realization. "A bastard son," he murmured, more to himself than to either of them. "I take it the warlord was not aware Zorvut was not true-born?"

"No, but unfortunately, the news spread quickly, and I was barely able to escape with my life," Kelvhan said. "I must assume that Hrul Bonebreaker has taken this to mean that the terms of the peace treaty are now null and void."

"Did Zorvut know?" Ruven asked sharply.

"No!" Taegan exclaimed, shaking his head. "No, he was just as shocked as I was to hear it. And... he was sad. It drove him to despair."

"Well, we don't know for sure," Kelvhan said, and Taegan whipped his head around to glare at him. "Forgive me, but we don't. He may have been shocked we found out, not at the news itself."

"You're wrong," Taegan replied, trying to sound forceful, but it came out as more of a plea. "You don't know anything about him. I'm telling you, he had no idea."

Through all this, the king remained silent, watching Taegan with an unreadable expression. His dark eyes were clouded with thought and his hand was pressed to his mouth.

"And he fled," he finally said in a low murmur, and Taegan glanced away from him, nodding. "He was afraid, and he fled." He took in a long, measured breath, releasing it in a slow exhale. "And the warlord intends to resume his war. Kelvhan, were you followed?"

"No, my king," he replied, bowing his head. "I am luckily strong enough to be able to magically return to a place I have been before, and retreated back to my home not an hour ago. I came here immediately."

"So we have a little while before they broach the border to fortify the capital. Hopefully, there is still enough time to defend the border villages." Ruven continued, more to himself than to the other two. Taegan wanted desperately to interject, to stand up for Zorvut, but he did not know what he could even say, so he held his tongue. But as if hearing his thoughts, Ruven looked sharply back over at him.

"My son," he said, his voice softening. "I know you care for Zorvut. But as it stands, this union was made under false pretenses, and no one would blame you for ending it."

"...Ending it?" Taegan repeated faintly. His heart, as much as it already ached, squeezed painfully at the king's suggestion.

"If you want," he continued tentatively. "And only if you want, I can sever the bond between you and nullify the marriage. Perhaps it is an extreme reaction, but if the worst-case scenario is true, and he fled back to his homeland for refuge, well... Perhaps it would be best for you two not to be linked."

"He didn't," Taegan protested, but doubt crept in even as he said it. What if he *had* known all along? What if it all truly had been a lie, a cruel trick, a long con to destroy Aefraya from within? He thought he had learned so much about Zorvut, but how could he be sure any of it was true? And even if it had been the truth, Zorvut had fled the castle, the city, perhaps never to return.

The king stepped forward to place a comforting hand on his shoulder. When he did, Taegan realized his whole body was trembling again.

"The decision is yours," he said softly. "But if it were mine, I would take every precaution. Your safety is my highest concern, Taegan."

"I understand," he replied, and squeezed his eyes shut to stop the flood of tears he could feel welling up behind them. "Okay. You're right. Do it."

Ruven peered at him closely, seeming to hesitate, before nodding and clasping one of Taegan's hands in his own. The other hand pressed against his face, the fingers splayed to rest along his forehead and temple, with the thumb nestled under his eye. He felt a warm tingle from the contact as the magic gathered beneath Ruven's fingertips, and closed his eyes. The king whispered an incantation, barely audible, and suddenly the warmth exploded into a searing heat that shot to the point in the back of his head like a homing beacon. It erupted into a burning pain and for a moment, all Taegan could see was red.

When his vision slowly returned, he realized he was on the ground, clutching the back of his head in agony. There were figures around him, more than there were a moment ago, but dimly he recognized the closest form as his father who was waving the others back.

"Taegan," he heard him saying quietly. "Taegan, you're alright. Can you speak?"

"Y-Yes," he gasped, the pain slowly receding, but still throbbing in his skull. It felt as if the sensation of a finger being crushed by a hammer had been condensed down into a needle and shoved into the nape of his neck. His lips were wet—he brushed them with his fingers and they came away a bright red. His nose was steadily dripping blood.

Immediately, regret flooded him. What had possessed him to agree to such a thing? The pain in his head was proof he had made a mistake, and he wondered fearfully if Zorvut had felt the same blossom of agony from their bond as it died. He supposed he would never find out now, and the thought sent a fresh pang of despair radiating from his heart to his fingertips.

King Ruven helped pull him to a sitting position, and he could more clearly see now that two guards who must have come rushing in from all the commotion had joined Kelvhan. One of the guards offered him a handkerchief, which he took and pressed to his nose. After a moment, he stood, his legs quivering beneath his weight.

"Try and get some rest," Ruven said in a low voice. Taegan could see in his eyes that he had not expected so visceral a reaction from him, though he was clearly trying to hide how shaken he was. "We'll talk more in the morning, but try and sleep."

"I can help him to his quarters, my king," Kelvhan interjected, and Ruven nodded in agreement. Taegan didn't have the strength to argue, so he wearily took Kelvhan's offered arm and allowed himself to be led from the room. Behind him be could hear his father speaking to the guards.

"Summon the generals to my study at once. We need to plan where to send scouts," he was saying, his voice growing more distant and faint as they walked. "And have the kitchens drop off a carafe of coffee. I doubt any of us will be sleeping tonight..."

He half-suspected Kelvhan to try to follow him to his room, but the other elf stopped short of his door when they arrived.

"I'm sorry, Taegan," he said, as Taegan pushed through the door. "I'm sorry it had to end up like this."

He had no reply to that, so he simply shut the door behind him without speaking. Somehow he managed to wash the blood from his face and find his way back to bed—the bed many sizes too big for him alone. Just a few hours ago they had gotten into bed together. His husband had held him in his arms—and now he was unbonded, unmarried.

He pressed his face into Zorvut's pillow and wept until a restless sleep took him.

# Chapter Twelve

In the morning, Taegan woke with his head throbbing and his eyes swollen. He lay motionless in bed for a long time, watching the empty spot where Zorvut would have been, before stumbling to the bathroom and splashing his face with warm water. Though he must have slept in fits and starts, he felt as if he had been wide awake all night.

He had no appetite, but lying alone in his room seemed suddenly detestable. When he opened his door, he spotted Aerik jumping to his feet from where it looked like he had been sitting across from the entrance.

"My prince," he said, his voice uncharacteristically nervous as he bowed his head. "I... I heard about last night. Please, is there anything I can do to assist you?"

Taegan opened his mouth to speak, but no noise came out. He swallowed hard, cleared his throat, and tried again.

"Will you bring me some tea to my study?" he asked hoarsely, and Aerik nodded quickly.

"Of course," he replied, and strode away. The sound of his footsteps echoed up from the spiral staircase. After a moment, Taegan forced himself to head down the stairs as well, making the short walk to his private study.

The curtains were open so the golden morning light shone through, illuminating the empty room. It would be a lovely morning, he thought as he curled up in his comfiest chair. It smelled a bit like Zorvut. He squeezed his eyes shut, but still felt a tear run down his face.

Taegan wasn't sure how long he sat there, but eventually he heard the door open and the clinking of dishes as Aerik returned with a kettle and a teacup on a platter. He opened his eyes to see the manservant ginger place the tray on the desk in front of him, and he nodded in thanks as he reached for the cup.

"My prince," Aerik said, with more emotion in his voice than Taegan could ever recall hearing from him. "I'm sorry. I don't know what to say." Taegan shook his head.

"Say nothing," he replied. "Sit with me for a bit."

Aerik nodded and sat down in one of the wooden chairs by Taegan's desk. His back remained stiff and straight, betraying his hesitance despite the carefully neutral expression on his face. Taegan looked away and instead watched the trees sway in the breeze through the window.

The tea had become lukewarm in his hands when a knock came at his study door. They both eyed the door before glancing at each other, and slowly Aerik rose to open it.

Kelvhan stood in the doorway as it swung open. The first tendril of emotion broke through the overwhelming numbness in Taegan's veins—his eyes narrowed in irritation.

"May I come in?" Kelvhan asked, looking past Aerik to meet Taegan's gaze across the room.

"Come in," he said, and added quickly, "Aerik, stay in here, please." They both paused in surprise; after a beat, Aerik stepped back into the room to clear the doorway, and Kelvhan slowly walked inside with a scowl.

"I was hoping to speak with you alone," he said in a measured tone. Taegan shrugged.

"If you cannot say it to me in front of my manservant, perhaps you should not say it at all," he replied, and Kelvhan sighed, stepping nearer to him.

"I did this for *you*, you know," he said softly. "All of this I did for you."

"For me?" Taegan said, sitting up and leaning forward, closer to the other elf. Kelvhan nodded. He seemed to hesitate for a brief moment, then extended a hand to lightly touch his shoulder.

"For us," he continued, barely above a whisper now. "Now there's nothing stopping us from being together."

"For *us*?" Taegan repeated incredulously, wrenching his shoulder out from Kelvhan's grasp. His tea splattered from the cup onto his fist and his lap, but he barely noticed.

"Of course I did it for us," he said, more forcefully this time. "But you should be grateful that the orc is gone. Gods, I couldn't stand it—"

"Shut up!" Taegan shouted, and Kelvhan took a rapid step back in surprise. Without realizing, Taegan was on his feet, quivering in rage. The teacup had fallen from his grasp and shattered on the floor. "Grateful? Is that how you think I should feel? I *told* you to stay away from me. I ordered you to leave us alone! Instead you've destroyed my marriage, sent our nation back into war, and for what? For nothing! I hate you! I *hate* you!"

"Taegan, please," Kelvhan hissed, glancing nervously between him and Aerik, who was still standing silently next to the door. But Taegan had never raised his voice like this, and now the floodgates were open.

"I said shut up!" he exclaimed. He sucked in a sharp breath and continued in a low, dangerous tone. "I don't know what possessed you to think this plan would work, but we will *never* be together. Especially not now. We were done the day I was married, and I made it clear I wanted you to leave me alone. It shouldn't matter whether Zorvut is a full orc or a half orc. I love him. Whatever you thought you might accomplish by getting between us, you won't. How many more of our people have you condemned to die now? You're going to leave my study, and leave the castle, and never return. If I ever, *ever* see you anywhere near me again, I'll have you killed. Get out."

Kelvhan stared at him, wide-eyed and mouth agape. All the color had drained from his face. They were silent for a beat, unmoving, then Taegan took an aggressive step closer to him.

"Get out!" he shouted, all the fury and rage and pain and despair that had coursed through him echoing through the stone hallways. This finally shook Kelvhan from his stupor, and he stumbled back toward the door. His face had quickly become red, whether in shame or anger Taegan couldn't tell.

"Fine," Kelvhan hissed, his lips pulled back in a hideous snarl. "I'll go. But if I can't have you, some filthy orc certainly won't. I promise you that." Before Taegan could reply, he had flung the door open and ran through it, slamming it behind him.

Taegan stood alone in the middle of the room for a long moment. He realized he was panting, his heart hammering in his chest and adrenaline flooding through him. He had to do something.

Aerik took a hesitant step toward him. "Are you alright, Prince Taegan?" he asked nervously, and gestured toward the shattered ceramic on the floor. "Please, allow me..."

Taegan took a step back and turned toward his desk. He had to do *something*, anything, to make this right. Shuffling through his things, he found a blank sheet of parchment and a quill, and began to scribble down a note.

*Father –*

*I must find Zorvut and bring him back to us. Ending our bond was a mistake. I know without a doubt he has no intention of betraying our trust, and fled in the fear of what you or I may have done to him when we learned the truth about his heritage. I regret sending him away and intend to leave immediately to find him and return him to safety. If you cannot accept him unless he is a true-born heir, then send us away when I return and we shall go without a fight. But without him, my heart is incomplete.*

*Taegan*

Hand trembling, he thrust the quill aside and folded up the note the moment he finished it, smudging some of the still-wet ink. Aerik was behind him, picking up the pieces of the broken cup.

"Aerik," he said sharply, and the other elf snapped to attention. "I need you to give this to my father as soon as you can." He placed the note in Aerik's hand and moved toward the exit.

"Of course," Aerik stammered, looking for the first time totally overwhelmed. "But, Prince Taegan, where are you going?"

"I don't know," he replied honestly, and was out the door. He ran to his room, throwing on a clean shirt, his riding breeches, and his boots, then hurried back out while tying his hair into a low ponytail. The castle halls were a blur of movement until he arrived at the stables, and the stable boy jumped up in surprise as he barged in.

"Prince Taegan!" the boy exclaimed, shock apparent on his face. "Forgive me, I didn't know you'd be riding today. Please, just a moment and I'll get Moonlight ready."

"No need," he said, barely looking at the boy as he strode past. "Were you here last night? Did you see Prince Zorvut leave?"

"No, my prince," the boy stammered. "I've only been on duty for an hour. But the last boy, he said he saw Prince Zorvut leave in a hurry in the middle of the night."

"Did he see him take anything when he left?"

"His greatsword, but other than that, just his riding gear, I think," he said, watching dumbfounded as Taegan began to saddle his horse. "Prince Taegan, what's going on?"

"I have to go," Taegan replied quickly. Moonlight whickered anxiously, sensing his nervous energy. "Bring me a traveling pack, with a waterskin and rations."

"Yes, of course," the boy exclaimed, scurrying away to find the items. It was sloppy work, but Taegan had Moonlight ready faster than he'd ever saddled a horse before in his life, and he led her out into the yard just as the stable boy was sprinting up, carrying a bedroll and backpack in his arms.

"Help me load up her saddlebags," he said, and the boy nodded rapidly, gasping for breath. Taegan hesitated, then stepped away. "Finish packing her. I'll be right back," he said, and he jogged across the field to the archery range. The largest longbow was missing from his personal cache, and a quiver. Zorvut must have taken it.

He slung his own bow over his shoulder, grabbing a full quiver, before running back to the stable. Jumping, he mounted Moonlight in one quick movement and took off, leaving the stable boy stammering and stumbling behind him.

"Open the gate!" he roared as he approached the castle gatehouse. He didn't think he could slow down if he wanted to. With a shout, the guards standing post at the gate leapt to action, flinging it open just in time for

Taegan to gallop through. He could hear them shouting for him, but he did not look back.

The main road out of the city was all cobblestone, so there were no prints to track. *Where would he have gone?* Taegan thought desperately as his eyes scanned the trail for any sign of Graksh't's massive hooves. Zorvut had appeared just as afraid of the warlord as he had been of the king, so it seemed unlikely he would go north toward the orc homeland. But he was unfamiliar with much of the area, and had only left the capital twice—the hunting trip with his father, and their hunting trip alone.

Their hunting trip. Surely he would have headed south, toward the Silverwood where the road eventually led into Autreth, to neutral land. He had a good twelve hour head start, but Taegan could catch up. He had to.

# Chapter Thirteen

Taegan rode south for over an hour with no sign of Zorvut or Graksh't. His head still throbbed, each pulse of pain a wave of doubt that he could ever find him. For all the certainty he had felt about where Zorvut would have fled, did he really know him that well after all? It was certainly where *he* would have gone, but Taegan didn't know if they were truly alike at all anymore. It was hopeless, he told himself, but he couldn't bring himself to turn Moonlight around. So onward he rode.

And then he saw it—just a flash of a print, much larger than Moonlight's. He thought he might have imagined it, but then there was another, and a line of them in a stretch of the dirt road that was muddy and soft. It had to be Graksh't. No other horse could leave a print so large. It had to be them.

"Yes," he heard himself breathe in relief, relaxing into the saddle for the first time since he'd set out.

He rode on. Eventually, Moonlight's pace slowed, and as much as he wanted to push her to maintain the same gallop, he knew the last thing he needed was to lose his horse, too. When he spotted Pondshear coming into view around the bend in the road, his heart leapt up into his throat, but there was no sign of the orc as he approached, only some muddy hoof prints continuing down the dirt pathway. By now, the sun had long since reached its peak and was beginning its descent back down toward the horizon in the west. His back ached, his thighs burned, his head still throbbed unendingly. But he couldn't stop. He had to catch up.

When the sun was low in the sky, he finally saw a tendril of smoke in the distance, a singular dot of light beneath it. It was coming from up ahead, a little way off the path.

"Please," Taegan whispered to himself, almost afraid to hope it was him as he rode toward it. As he drew nearer, the faint shapes became clearer. A campfire, a tent, a massive horse—and an orc with a greatsword strapped to his back.

"*Zorvut!*" he shouted with every ounce of strength left in him, standing in his stirrups. The figure whirled around to face him, reaching reflexively for the greatsword on his back. As he turned, he could see Zorvut's fierce, battle-ready expression morph into shock as he recognized Taegan galloping toward him. It felt as though he were moving in slow motion, unable to get to him fast enough.

"Taegan?" he asked incredulously once he was within earshot. "What are you doing here?"

Taegan pulled back on the reins and Moonlight slowed to a stop a few paces away. Leaping off her in one quick motion, he moved to close the gap between them, but Zorvut stepped away hesitantly.

"I had to find you," Taegan said as he stopped, realizing he was panting for breath. "This was a mistake. I'm so sorry, Zorvut, please, you have to come back."

Zorvut's brows furrowed, his lips pressing together in a grim line. He lifted a hand as if he wanted to pull Taegan close to him, then turned away.

"You should go back home," he said, a forced coldness in his voice as he stepped toward his campfire.

"Not without you," Taegan insisted, following him. "Please, I made a mistake. Did you..." He swallowed hard, forcing down the fear that welled in his throat. "Did you feel it, in your head, last night?"

Zorvut stopped when he said it, instinctively reaching up to touch the spot where his skull met his neck. All pretense of tough aloofness was gone now.

"Yes," he said softly. "I'm sorry."

"No, I made a mistake. It was me," Taegan said, causing Zorvut to look back at him in confusion. "When you left, I... We talked to my father, and he suggested severing the bond, and... It was a moment of weakness, but I accepted. I never should have done it, I regretted it immediately. I'm so sorry."

For a long moment Zorvut stared at him silently, processing his words.

"Severing the bond?" he repeated slowly.

"Yes," Taegan replied, nodding. The anguish in his voice was palpable. "The bond between us was cut. We're unbonded... Unmarried."

Zorvut blinked, and Taegan saw a tear fall down his face as he looked away.

"I thought it was me," Zorvut said softly, shaking his head. "I thought I had gone too far from you, and... And that's just what the distance was like."

"No, it was me. It was my fault," he interrupted, fighting back his own tears. "I'm so sorry. Please, Zorvut, I beg you, come home."

"I *can't*," Zorvut insisted, pressing a hand to his eyes. "It's not safe. Not for either of us."

"I can't go home without you."

"You can. You will."

"I can't!" Taegan exclaimed, shaking his head. "Because I—I love you, Zorvut. I'm in love with you."

Time froze as Zorvut's golden-yellow eyes met his in surprise. He had wanted to say so much more, but the words stuck in his throat and his confession hung heavy in the air between them. When Zorvut finally spoke, it was in a soft, hoarse whisper.

"Taegan..." he said, looking away. That was all it took for the floodgates to open.

"I love you," Taegan repeated. His voice broke as he began to cry openly. "Please come home with me. I want to marry you again, this time for love, if nothing else. I don't care about the terms of the peace treaty, I care about you. None of it matters to me, Zorvut, I just want *you*. Please."

He wiped the tears from his eyes and looked away, unable to meet Zorvut's gaze out of fear. Had he come all this way only to be rejected?

"Taegan," he heard Zorvut say again, and suddenly he was enveloped in his arms, being pressed tight to his chest. A ragged sob escaped Taegan's lips as he held on desperately. "I love you, too, Taegan."

The relief that flooded through him at those words was incandescent. All the exhaustion left him at once, like unhooking a heavy cloak and dropping it to the floor. He nodded against Zorvut's chest, unable to formulate words as they embraced.

"I was so afraid," Zorvut continued, his voice rumbling through his chest against Taegan's ear. "I was so afraid you would be harmed. I just wanted you to be safe, I never wanted to hurt you."

"I won't let them," Taegan finally said through his tears, reaching up to cup Zorvut's face in his hands. "I won't let them hurt either of us." He pulled his face down to his own and kissed him hard. Nothing mattered but the contact between them, Zorvut's arms wrapped tightly around him and their lips moving against each other. Though they had been apart only a day, they kissed as passionately as if they had been separated for months.

When they finally broke the kiss, one of Zorvut's hands came up to run his fingers through Taegan's hair, the other still embracing him.

"You'll come home?" Taegan asked in a whisper, closing his eyes. He felt Zorvut nod as their foreheads pressed together.

"I will," he affirmed, and kissed his forehead.

"You'll marry me again?"

"I will."

"You love me?"

"I love you."

"Show me," Taegan breathed, and slipped his hands underneath Zorvut's shirt.

Before he could even get the shirt unfastened, Zorvut was lifting him up and carrying him to the tent. They descended in a tumble to his bedroll, Taegan's legs straddling Zorvut's waist below him.

"I love you," he breathed as Zorvut's hands traced across his body, brushing against his nipples and pressing into the divot of his hips. "I love you, I love you." Zorvut only responded in a low, rumbling growl, but the insistence of his erection pressed against Taegan was answer enough.

He kicked his breeches off, stripping naked quickly as Zorvut undressed leisurely, his eyes running up and down Taegan's body. Even though he could not feel Zorvut's desire directly, the heat in his gaze still sent a jolt of arousal straight to his cock.

Before Zorvut could fully undress, Taegan leaned down and kissed him again. They kissed lazily for a moment until Zorvut broke apart to pull off his shirt, only to join their lips anew, then he whimpered against Zorvut's mouth as the head of his cock pressed firmly against him. He was already slick with arousal and sank easily onto his cock, his head tilting back with a moan. Zorvut pressed his lips instead to his neck, kissing along his jaw and collarbones as he moved slowly, relishing in the long, slow strokes sliding in and out of him. The familiar fullness of Zorvut reaching the deepest parts of him spread through his abdomen as he took him down to the hilt, sending tiny shock waves of pleasure coursing through his whole body—he could never be satisfied with anyone else. He moved his hips in a slow, careful movement, and hissed in pleasure as Zorvut took his cock in his hand, stroking it in time with his hips.

"So big," he groaned, watching the slight swell of his belly where Zorvut filled him to the brim. Pleasure burned through every vein in his body, and his own cock all but disappearing in Zorvut's hand drove him to the edge. "Fuck, I'm already—ahh!" His eyes squeezed shut as he came, and he cried aloud as Zorvut stroked him harder, milking every drop of come into a warm pool on his belly. It was not as earth-shattering as the climaxes they shared through the bond, but there was still a familiarity to the heat that coursed through him.

His eyes fluttered open as Zorvut's hands released him and moved along his body again, sending sharp pulses of pleasure through his sensitized nerves. One hand came to rest on his back, pushing him down to lean into Zorvut's torso, the other clasping his ass and spreading him wider, feeling along the place where their bodies conjoined. Now Zorvut's hips were moving, thrusting in and out of him, and Taegan let out a muffled moan against his shoulder, wrapping his arms around his neck.

"Gods, you feel so good," Zorvut groaned in his ear. "I can't—I don't want to hurt you."

"Don't hold back," Taegan begged, eliciting a helpless moan from Zorvut as his hips stuttered. "Harder."

He didn't need to ask again, as Zorvut immediately began to fuck him harder, grabbing his hips with both hands as he thrust up into him. Pain and pleasure exploded through him in equal parts at the rapid, unbearable fullness, and he dug his fingernails into Zorvut's neck as he cried out.

The friction of their bodies pressed together and the warm slickness of his own come against his overstimulated cock drove him to orgasm again rapidly; only a few weak spurts of come left him but the pleasure coursed through his body all the same, leaving him twitching and pulsating around Zorvut's cock.

"My Taegan," Zorvut moaned as Taegan clenched around him. "My love. You're mine—you're *mine*." The last word was a growl accentuated with one last hard thrust, and Taegan gasped as a hot gush of liquid filled his belly, stretching him open even more. He could feel Zorvut's cock pulsating inside him as he came, his load filling him to the brim and dripping out of him in excess.

They lay together for a long time, still joined as they caught their breath, Zorvut's hands trailing soft, shapeless lines in a comforting gesture along Taegan's back. Finally he shifted his hips and Taegan whined as the cock slid out of him, only for the sound to morph into a moan as a lewd gush of liquid followed, the come dripping from him in a thick, steady stream.

"Gods, what am I going to do with you?" Zorvut muttered, watching in half-aroused fascination as his seed spilled out of Taegan's body.

"You've ruined me for anyone else," Taegan teased, then kissed along his neck. A breathy sigh escaped

Zorvut's lips at the contact. "So you've got to fuck me every day. That's what you're going to do with me."

"I already want you again," Zorvut groaned. For the first time, there was a needy whine to his voice much like Taegan's own, and a pleased grin spread across his face.

"Eventually, *I'm* going to fuck *you*," he said as he pulled Zorvut up into a sitting position. "But for now, I suppose you can have me again."

# Chapter Fourteen

They rose late the next morning, wrapped comfortably in warm blankets beneath the tent. There was an unspoken understanding that whatever the day held for them upon their return was likely to be far less pleasant than their time spent alone here. Much as he wished the morning would last forever, Taegan roused himself to start a small meal as Zorvut packed up his belongings.

"Where were you headed?" Taegan asked curiously as he watched him disassemble the tent. Zorvut shrugged.

"Truth be told, I'm not sure," he said. "I think I would have continued south into Autreth if I could, to find sanctuary there."

"Not a bad idea," Taegan said. He wanted to add that it would be a good option if they could not return to the capital, but couldn't bring himself to speak it aloud.

Once they had packed everything away, they set out on the road, heading north back toward the castle.

At their leisurely pace, Taegan estimated they would arrive back at Castle Aefraya shortly after sunset.

It was strange, being so close to Zorvut yet unable to feel him in his head through the bond. There was still some pain, which had steadily receded over time, but it was a constant reminder of his mistake. He would never be so rash again.

Though there were snippets of conversation throughout the day, they mostly rode in silence. Despite the uncertainty of what would await them when they reached their destination, Taegan was just glad to be riding alongside him at all.

Well past midday, the little fishing village of Pondshear came into view. A small smile played at Taegan's lips at the sight of it, but quickly morphed into a frown as a faint, distant shout pierced the air. It was coming from the direction of the village. His head snapped to look at Zorvut, who met his gaze, looking equally surprised.

"You heard it too?" he asked.

"Let's go," Zorvut replied with a nod, and they quickened their pace toward the village.

More shouts joined in as they got closer, and the unmistakable sound of steel striking steel.

"You don't think it could be a war party already?" Taegan exclaimed as Zorvut galloped ahead. His bow had been slung across his back, but he pulled it out in anticipation of a fight.

"Why would they be this far south?" Zorvut replied without looking back at him, but he didn't sound convinced. With everything that had happened already, it would be far-fetched, but not impossible for a party of orcs, maybe a small band of scouts, to have arrived within the kingdom's borders. Who else would attack a sleepy fishing village?

Sure enough, as they approached and more of the village came into view, Taegan could make out the hulking figures of four orcs on horseback, skirmishing with what looked to be two guards and a handful of lay people armed with makeshift weapons. The orcs had circled around the elves, harrying them into a tight group.

Instinctively, Taegan drew an arrow and loosed it in the direction of the largest orc of the group. It whistled through the air and missed the orc as they cantered, but struck his enormous horse in its haunches, causing it to rear up with a scream. That grabbed the orc's attention—he pointed at them and bellowed, and the other three caught sight of them, too.

"Stay behind me," Zorvut growled, drawing his sword as he galloped on ahead. Taegan slowed, cantering further down the road as Zorvut barreled into the fray.

"Traitor!" the larger orcs roared at him as they moved to meet his approach. The pair of elves looked around in bewilderment as their attackers seemed to forget about them entirely. "Half-blood!"

Zorvut did not respond, only swung his greatsword at them as they approached. The weapon was easily as long as Taegan was tall, yet he maneuvered it in one hand and held his horse's reins in the other effortlessly. In one fell swoop, the first orc to approach him howled in pain as Zorvut feinted to the side and slashed him in the ribs, dark blood staining the blade.

Taegan was transfixed for only a moment at how natural and easy Zorvut made it look despite the size advantage the others had on him, then shook himself to his senses to draw another arrow. Zorvut circled back around, but one of the orcs was getting close, too close—Taegan aimed his sights at that one, and embedded an arrow deep in his shoulder. He looked in the direction of the arrow and caught sight of Taegan, an expression of unbridled fury crossing over his face. He drew another arrow rapidly, shooting this one into the orc's chest. The orc winced, but did not stop as he galloped toward Taegan.

Fear gripped him as he kicked into Moonlight's sides, sending her bolting, but he knew the larger legs of the orc's warhorse would catch up to him quickly. He had not even brought his sword with him in his hurry to leave the day before—the only close-range weapon he had was the dagger in his belt, useless when the orc had such longer reach with his ax. The orc charging him roared something he did not understand. He twisted back to fire another arrow at him—the angle was bad, he moved too hastily to get a good look, and he missed.

"Taegan!" Zorvut shouted, and Taegan caught sight of him breaking free from the group, galloping toward him. One of the orcs now lay unmoving on the ground, but the other two were close behind him.

The charging orc was upon him now, swinging an ax that missed him by a hair's breadth. He loosed another arrow, but the orc had the advantage of being behind him, and it grazed the orc's ear but went sailing on past him. When he looked, the orc's eyes were not on him but on Moonlight—with a shout, he wrenched his feet out of his stirrups. The ax came down again and Taegan was tumbling to the ground, Moonlight shrieking in pain.

"No!" he wailed in a panic even as he skidded through the damp earth. "No!" He had freed himself from the saddle just in time and was not wounded, but his bow clattered out of reach and the ground beneath them was streaked with red. Moonlight had fallen next to him, blood gushing from her hind leg. But he couldn't look at her long—the sound of hooves pounding into the dirt circled around him and drew closer.

"*Taegan!*" Zorvut's voice came, just out of his view. Taegan instinctively raised his hands above his head, an ineffective shield against the hulking form bearing down on him.

A roar of *something* filled the air, and in an instant, a flash of heat and light streaked through the sky and slammed into the orc's chest, knocking him from his horse with a pained shout. He fell to the ground, howling as the arrows stuck in him were on fire, more flames licking along his clothes.

"What?" Taegan panted, staring in shock at the incapacitated orc. "Who...?"

He looked, and Zorvut was a few yards away from him, still atop his horse with an equally stunned expression, looking down at his hand which cupped a ball of flickering flame. But he seemed to snap out of it quickly and looked back to Taegan.

"Get behind me," he said as he rode up, and Taegan clambered to his feet. The two orcs who had been pursuing him had come to an uneasy halt, staring with distrust at the flames in Zorvut's hand. The two elven guards must have ushered away the common folk caught up in the skirmish and were now approaching cautiously, one with a crossbow and the other with a sword. They looked questioningly at Taegan, and he held up a hand for them to wait.

"Traitor," the orc on the ground groaned, having wrenched the burning arrows out of his body. Taegan realized with a start that the orc was speaking *elvish-* —whatever he was going to say, he wanted the elves to hear him and understand. The flames that had crept along his clothing were now mostly extinguished as he glared up at them from the dirt. His spooked horse had dashed away and did not seem to be slowing. "Whatever mercy Hrul may have had on you, half-breed, it's gone now. He will know of your treason and cut you down with the rest of them. This will *all* be orcish land again before long."

"Good to know," Zorvut replied coldly, still holding the fire in his hand as he looked down at the wounded orc from his horse. "Flee, then, and warn the warlord that any other scouts he may send here will meet the same fate as your friend, or worse." He turned to face the other two orcs still on their horses, a cruel scowl spreading across his face. "Go!" he bellowed, and with a start, they began to gallop away, heading for the bridge to the other side of the river. The wounded orc lumbered to his feet and chased after them, apparently abandoning his horse.

His horse. With a sob, Taegan ran to Moonlight's motionless form on the ground. She whickered weakly as he stumbled to his knees next to her head, but did not move. A puddle of blood surrounded them. Now that he was close enough to have a good look, the ax had cut her down to the bone. Tears sprang to his eyes as he looked away, unable to bear the gruesome sight—it was undoubtedly a mortal wound, and she was fading quickly.

"Taegan," Zorvut's voice came softly—he was already next to him, kneeling in the dirt at his side. "I'm so sorry."

Taegan nodded wordlessly, unable to make a sound around the lump in his throat. He gently stroked Moonlight's face, running his fingers through her mane. Her eyes followed the movement for a moment until her eyelids slowly shut. It felt like only an instant until she was gone.

In light of everything that had happened, it seemed such a small thing to shed tears over. But he could not stop himself from weeping as her breaths slowed and stopped. Zorvut pulled him into his arms and he pressed his face into his shoulder, stifling his cries.

But there was still work to be done. He allowed himself his moment of weakness and wept bitterly into Zorvut's shoulder, then forced himself to pull away, wiping his eyes and breathing deeply until the tears stopped.

"Are you all right?" he asked hoarsely, gingerly holding his fingers to Zorvut's arm where he had been wounded.

"Just a scratch," Zorvut reassured him, pressing his hand over the cut. It came away bloody, but it did seem to be a shallow wound. Taegan nodded, and shakily stood, Zorvut steadying him. The two elven guards had approached but were still standing a careful distance away, and he could see some of the lay folk who had been caught up in the commotion now peeking their heads out of their homes to watch.

"Prince Taegan," one of the guards said cautiously, her eyes flitting between Taegan and Zorvut as if unsure who to watch more closely. Her fair hair had been pulled back in a tight bun, but some pieces of it had fallen loose in the skirmish and were now plastered to her perspiring face. "Are you all right?"

"Yes," he replied with a nod, leaning against Zorvut's steady frame. "What happened here?"

"They came out of nowhere, my prince," she replied. "I'm not even sure where they crossed the river, as we didn't see anyone coming from the bridge. By the time we saw them they were already nearly in the town square." She hesitated, glancing away. "We had heard rumors yesterday, but... I take it this means the peace treaty is really over? Are we at war again?"

The despair in her tone was enough to make Taegan feel as though his heart might shatter once more. These were his people, his responsibility, and he had promised them a new age of peace only to have their vision destroyed. How many had she known who had already died on the battlefield, and how many more would follow?

"Unfortunately, that seems to be the case," he replied in a dark tone, forcing himself to meet her gaze. "But let me assure you of this. Whatever rumors you may have heard, my trust in my husband remains unwavering. He has no intention of betraying us, and that is the truth, just as you saw."

He felt Zorvut's breath hitch as the words *my husband* left his lips. His hand on Taegan's shoulder gave a gentle, reassuring squeeze. The guard looked between them a moment longer, then nodded.

"Thank you for your help here, Prince Zorvut," she said, giving a polite bow of her head as she addressed him. "Without you, I fear we may have been overpowered."

"I'm glad to be of service," Zorvut replied, nodding solemnly. "I only wish things had not turned out this way."

"Prince Taegan," the other guard offered, finally speaking up. "If you have a need for a horse to return home, I'm sure we can find one suitable for you. It would be our honor."

The offer was like a fistful of salt in the open wound of his heart, but Taegan nodded, hoping it was not obvious on his face.

"That would be much appreciated," he said, then looked back at Moonlight's body. "Is there somewhere we can bury her?"

The guards glanced at each other, hesitating until the woman, who seemed to be in charge, spoke up.

"If you'd prefer, we can have her body taken to the castle, if you wanted to bury her somewhere there," she said, but Taegan shook his head.

Moonlight had been a gift from his late father, not long before he had died. It seemed somehow fitting to him for her to be laid to rest at the place he was born.

"No, I'd like to leave her here," he said.

"There's a good spot just a bit south," the other guard interjected. "A nice sunny hill with a view of the river."

"That would be nice," Taegan agreed, nodding. "Thank you."

Together, he and Zorvut removed the saddle bags and other equipment from Moonlight's still body. At first, he had been worried how they would move her, but Zorvut seemed to have little issue shifting her weight as they dragged away the saddle.

"I can carry her," he said gruffly once everything had been removed.

"Wait!" Taegan exclaimed, and Zorvut froze. He pulled out his dagger and found a braid in her mane that was not bloodstained, and cut it cleanly near the root. Pensively, he wrapped the lock of hair around his fingers, feeling its softness for a moment, before carefully pocketing it and sheathing his blade. Zorvut gave him a nod of understanding when their eyes met.

"All right," he relented, then added in concern, "Don't hurt yourself."

"I won't," Zorvut reassured him. He bent his knees, pushed his hands under her body near the ribs and haunches, took in a deep breath, and with a groan of exertion, stood straight with the body in his arms. He took a moment to secure his grip, then in one quick motion, slung the horse across one shoulder. It was clearly a struggle, but doable, and he began to take heavy, measured steps toward the hill the guard had pointed out. Taegan watched in awe, love and sadness swelling in his heart in equal measure.

The two guards brought shovels and helped them dig, conversing briefly, but mostly remaining in silence. The woman, Tessa, explained they were the only guards posted at the tiny fishing village; she had only been assigned here last year, but the man, Aldwin, had been in the village all his life.

"I actually met the King-Consort a handful of times," he said as they dug, his voice curt yet hesitant. "He was nearly an adult when I was young, and moved to the castle before I was a teen, but I always liked him and his family. He was a good man."

"Yes, he was," Taegan agreed softly with a nod. He didn't dare look away from the fresh earth he was methodically digging into, for fear he might start to cry again.

Once a sufficient grave had been dug, the four of them stood over it for a long moment. Tessa gingerly touched Aldwin's arm, whispering something, and they took a few steps back to give them space.

"I'll get her," Zorvut said, setting his shovel down. This time he half-lifted, half-pushed the horse, and she fell unceremoniously into the grave. Her mane was still braided, though the clean white of it was now stained with blood and dirt. She deserved more, Taegan thought sadly, but this was the most they could do for her.

"She was a good horse, and a faithful companion. My Papa gifted her to me when she was just a foal," he murmured. Zorvut placed an arm around his waist, steady and comforting. He tried to say more but choked on the words. Wiping his eyes, he managed, "Goodbye, Moonlight."

Decisively, he tossed the first shovelful of soil back over her, and after a moment Zorvut joined in as well, then the other two elves.

When she was buried, the group stood in silence for a long time, then Taegan turned wordlessly to return to the village. He did not look to see if the others followed.

Back in the town square, Graksh't had been tethered to a pole, and a white and chestnut paint horse had been brought out and was tethered next to him. Moonlight's saddle and equipment were all affixed to the horse, which occasionally huffed and eyed Graksh't nervously. A young woman, no more than perhaps nineteen or twenty, was standing and braiding its mane. Her long ashy brown hair was pulled back in a high ponytail, and she wore a green tunic and weathered, mud-stained boots over plain breeches. When she noticed Taegan approaching, she jumped away from the horse and lowered her head, clearly nervous.

"My prince," she said breathlessly. "I've brought you my horse. She's called Pippy, she's small but very friendly and reliable, and I—I hope she'll serve you well. I saw the beautiful braids on your mare, and, well, these aren't as good, but..." She trailed off, her face reddening as she looked away.

"I appreciate your generosity," Taegan said as graciously as he could manage. "I'm sure Pippy will prove to be just as excellent as you've described. And what's your name?"

"I'm Elincia," she replied, her head still bowed.

"Elincia," Taegan repeated. "I promise you Pippy will be returned safely, and you'll be compensated for the trouble."

"Oh, no, I'm honored just to help," Elincia exclaimed, finally looking up at him in surprise. "I didn't—I don't expect anything in return, my prince. I just work in the stable, and I know Pippy rides well with just about everyone."

"Please," Taegan replied firmly, placing his hand over hers where she gripped the reins. "It's the least we can do."

The girl hesitated, but finally gave a nod of affirmation.

"Okay," she agreed, and her gaze flitted past Taegan for a brief moment. He could feel Zorvut approaching behind him. She lowered her head, eyes dropping to the ground. "Thank you, my prince."

"It's you I should thank," he said, and managed a wry smile, which she returned nervously as she stepped away.

He climbed onto the saddle of this new horse—as the girl had told him, Pippy seemed to be a friendly and patient mare, giving Taegan no fuss as they set out once again. She was not Moonlight, but she could get him back home.

They were a little way down the road, the village disappearing behind them, when Taegan finally turned to him and asked, "What... What was that?"

He did not need to elaborate—the moment he said it, Zorvut nervously glanced down at his hands gripping the reins.

"I don't know," he replied, his voice a frightened whisper.

"That *was* you, right?" Taegan asked, still looking at him.

"Yes. I mean, I think so," Zorvut answered, though he sounded uncertain. "I just... I don't know, I knew I couldn't get to you in time, but I wanted to protect you. It was all I could think about, that I just needed to keep you safe. And I reached out to try and get to you, and... That happened. Gods, I used magic." His tone was as incredulous as if he were claiming to fly.

"You did," Taegan agreed, though he was just as bewildered. "That's never happened before?"

"I swear on my life, not once," he said, shaking his head. "Orcs with magic are so rare, they're made shamans or druids the moment they start showing any affinity for it. I had no idea I could do that." He frowned, and held out one of his hands in front of him, staring intently at it—but nothing happened, and he lowered his hand with a sigh. "I don't even know how I did it. I just... *did.*"

"Well," Taegan said slowly, unsure if he wanted to bring it up now, of all times. "Your mother did say it was a human... Perhaps he had some ability for magic, and now it's been passed down to you?"

Zorvut frowned, the thought clearly still distasteful to him. It was too soon for such a suggestion after all, but he couldn't take it back now. "I suppose that's the most likely possibility," he agreed, sighing. "But, well... It's still the least of our concerns for today, I think. Maybe we can investigate later."

"Later," Taegan conceded with a nod. Hopefully, he thought, there *would* be a later.

# Chapter Fifteen

A cold numbness had fallen over him for the remainder of their journey, but as the silhouette of the castle became visible in the sky, streaked with the colors of sunset, a bolt of anxiety burst through Taegan's heart. For all his brave words back at the village, it was still entirely possible the king would deny him entry. Part of him did not truly think his father would turn them away, but it seemed there was little he could rely on as the truth anymore.

Evidently, Zorvut did not need the bond to sense his mounting nervousness. He and Graksh't were a few paces ahead of him, as the little paint horse had a smaller stride and seemed nervous when she was very close to the much larger stallion. But he slowed enough to trot alongside Taegan as the castle came into view.

"Taegan," he said in a low voice. "Just... no matter what happens, we'll be together."

"We will," Taegan agreed, nodding. That, at least, he could be sure was the truth.

As they approached the gates, he could see the guards jump in surprise as they recognized him. They seemed to hesitate, then one hurried away, heading into the guard tower adjoining the gate. Another began to walk toward them, a worried expression on his face.

"Prince Taegan," he said, nodding politely at him, before hesitating and also bowing his head toward Zorvut. "And Prince Zorvut. Welcome."

That seemed like a good sign, if nothing else. Taegan glanced at Zorvut, who appeared to think the same thing, and nodded as well.

"The King requested that if we were to see you, to send you on to him immediately," the guard continued. He walked quickly alongside their horses now as they drew closer to the gate of the city. His eyes had lingered on Pippy, recognizing that it was not the same horse Taegan had left the city on, but he continued to walk with them without commenting on it. "He was, ah, quite insistent, my prince."

"Good thing I already planned to do so," Taegan replied, as the gates swung open before them. The guard seemed nervous and distressed at the sight of them, but not in the manner Taegan would have expected. Whatever that meant, he was uncertain.

There was a strange disquiet to the streets as they made their way uphill toward the castle walls. The townsfolk were out and about, but some of the bustle of the city seemed to be lacking somehow—or perhaps they just fell quiet when they saw Taegan and Zorvut approach. He could feel their eyes following him, but no one called out or raised their hand in greeting.

This time, as they reached the castle gates, they were already open and the guard standing watch ushered them through. One of the guards on the wall must have gone ahead to announce their arrival. The moment they were on the castle grounds, though, the gate began to close behind them, and two stable hands approached to take their horses.

"You didn't take Moonlight, my prince?" one asked in confusion as Taegan dismounted from the paint horse. He winced, and he could see Zorvut flinch out of the corner of his eye as well.

"I did," he replied, and the stable hand immediately reddened, looking away in embarrassment as he seemed to grasp the situation. "Tomorrow, please have this horse returned to a girl named Elincia in Pondshear, along with a hundred gold pieces for her trouble."

"Yes, my prince," he stammered, still unable to meet Taegan's gaze.

Once the horses had been taken away, all that was left to enter the castle.

"Seems like only good omens so far," Zorvut said quietly as they started up the stone steps to the main entrance.

"It does," Taegan agreed. "I don't want to get my hopes up, though." Zorvut touched the small of his back gingerly from below him on the steps, a reassuring gesture.

When they arrived in the foyer, a servant was already walking up to them.

"King Ruven is in the throne room, Prince Taegan," she said, quiet but urgent, her eyes trained carefully on the ground.

"Let's go, then," Taegan said, gripping Zorvut's hand. He squeezed back, and for a brief moment, his anxiety was quelled.

Together they walked down the right-hand hallway to the throne room; the door was closed, but did not look like it was locked. Taegan glanced at Zorvut, who nodded, before taking a deep breath and pushing the door open.

Inside, King Ruven was sitting atop the alabaster throne, a handful of other elves standing around him. Taegan recognized some as local nobles, generals in the army, and advisors—there had been a quiet murmur of conversation that fell silent as the door opened. Ruven's head snapped in the door's direction, and he immediately stood when he caught sight of them.

"Taegan!" he exclaimed, and the crowd parted as he leapt down from the raised platform and walked—no, *ran*—toward Taegan.

"Father," Taegan stammered, his eyes wide, hardly able to react before the king threw his arms around him, pressing them together tightly.

"I was so worried," his voice came, muffled against Taegan's shoulder. "My son. My son. I was so worried about you."

"I'm sorry to have frightened you," Taegan replied softly, and lifted his arms to hug his father back. Part of him had known the king surely would not have cast them out. It had been drowned out by his uncertainty and fear, but now all his anxiety had melted away.

After a long moment, Ruven finally pulled away, holding Taegan by his shoulders to look him up and down. His eyes were gleaming with unshed tears, sending a pang of guilt through Taegan's heart. Ruven had only ever treated him with love and kindness. How could he have ever doubted his own father?

"You're not hurt, then?" he asked, then looked up at Zorvut, a tight smile spreading across his face. "And you found him. I'm glad."

"Yes," Taegan answered, nodding. "I found him. I'm not hurt. But..." He hesitated, glancing away. "We witnessed an orc attack on the fishing village on our way home today, and... Moonlight was slain."

The king's brows furrowed in a pained expression.

"I'm sorry," he said softly, pulling Taegan closer to embrace him again. "Papa's last gift to you... I know you loved her dearly."

Taegan nodded wordlessly. He knew that if he said anything else about her, he would almost certainly burst into tears once more.

When Ruven pulled away this time, he glanced back at the group of advisors who were waiting quietly near the throne, politely looking everywhere except where the three of them stood in the entrance way.

"Forgive the interruption," King Ruven said loudly. "If you don't mind, let us take a short recess of an hour or two. I must speak to my son in private." He glanced at Zorvut and added privately, "And you, of course, Zorvut."

Zorvut nodded silently, and the group of advisors all murmured their assent as well.

"Come," the king said, stepping past them out of the throne room. "Let us speak in my private study."

Taegan glanced at Zorvut, who gave a slight nod. He had remained silent, but his expression seemed cautiously optimistic. Taegan reached out to take his hand again, and they followed Ruven out of the chamber.

When they arrived at the king's private study, his servant was stationed outside and silently acknowledged them with a nod. Ruven did not send him away, but closed the door behind him as they entered.

"Taegan," he said quietly as the door closed and he looked up to meet their eyes. "I am so, so sorry. To both of you." He hesitated, then bowed deeply before both of them. Taegan's heart leapt up into his throat, almost in a panic—he had never seen his father, the king, make such a contrite gesture before, and he had no idea how to respond. "Please forgive the part I played in all of this."

"Ah, that's—I mean, well, thank you, and I accept your apology," he stammered, then glanced at Zorvut. "We both do."

Zorvut hesitated, then nodded as well. "Yes," he agreed.

"Zorvut," the king said, looking at him as he straightened. "I owe you an individual apology. Taegan had faith in you, but I doubted, and made him doubt as well. But I see now that he trusts you implicitly, and from here on out, so will I. My son loves you, and that is more than enough for me."

Zorvut's expression seemed almost pained as the king spoke, but he did not break eye contact.

"Thank you," he finally replied in a low, gravelly voice—Taegan realized with a start that he was on the verge of tears. "I was... I confess, I did not trust you either, in that moment. I was afraid. But I made things worse by leaving. If you will have me, it would honor me to join you, and fight at your side."

"We will need all the help we can get, I'm afraid," the king answered wryly, sighing. "This morning, we received a formal declaration of war from the Bonebreaker clan. It all seems rather foolish to me; even with this, ah, new information we have learned, we would not have made an attack on them. The spirit of the peace treaty was upheld, after all."

"My father needs little reason to start a fight," Zorvut said bitterly, then seemed to catch himself, wincing. "The warlord, that is. I would imagine he is angry, and has no other use for his anger."

"We should have a discussion about all this, as I would appreciate hearing your input," Ruven continued. "But first, I... The more pressing matter should be to reinstate your bond. If you would like it, that is."

"Yes," Taegan blurted, then caught himself and glanced at Zorvut, who seemed to bite back a laugh. "I think we both would like that."

"Yes, I would," Zorvut agreed softly.

"I can summon the high priest now," Ruven said, and Taegan gave a start of surprise. "To be frank, I was afraid to tell anyone about... breaking the bond, for fear it might cause further upset in all of this. So no one knows but us, and that sorcerer, Kelvhan."

A tinge of acrid bile rose in Taegan's throat at the very mention of Kelvhan's name, but he did not want to get into it then. But when he did explain Kelvhan's cruel motives, he was sure his father would be just as enraged as he was.

"Right now?" Zorvut asked, bringing him back to the moment. There would be time to make a formal report of everything later; now, all Taegan could bring himself to care about was their bond.

"Is that alright?" Ruven asked. "It would be a private affair this time, just us and the high priest."

Taegan and Zorvut looked at each other. They were both tired and dirty, a bloody bandage still around Zorvut's arm. Their worn travel clothes would make a stark contrast to the finery they had worn the first time, and Taegan couldn't help but laugh.

"Yes, have him summoned," he said with a chuckle. "Why don't we go have a quick wash and change into something clean, and then we will come right back?"

"That's reasonable," Ruven said with a dry smile. "In that case, why don't we meet in the temple in an hour? Is that sufficient?"

"I think so," Taegan said. "Zorvut?"

"An hour," he agreed, nodding.

"Go on, then," the king said, waving his hand at the door. "I'll go speak with the high priest."

They left the private study and made the familiar walk back to their quarters. It was strange, how different everything felt even though they walked the same stairways and halls they had traversed so many times before. Taegan did not know if it was due to the dark backdrop of war after such brief but blissful peace, or the anticipation of reinstating their bond, or maybe both.

As they ascended the spiral staircase to their rooms, Taegan could hear the shuffling footsteps of Aerik. The servant must have been keeping watch for him, as he was standing directly in front of the staircase as they emerged, and he visibly sighed in relief as Taegan came into view.

"My prince," he said breathlessly. "You found him."

"I did," Taegan said, and could not help the pleased smile that spread across his face. "Will you draw us a bath? It's been a long journey."

"Of course," Aerik said, hurrying toward the door.

"And, Aerik," he added, holding up his hand. Aerik paused, looking over at him expectantly. "...Thank you. For everything." He blinked in surprise, then smiled.

"It's my pleasure, Prince Taegan. Prince Zorvut," he said, and strode ahead.

"Well, *Prince* Zorvut," Taegan said as they entered the room. "What would you like to see me wear to our wedding?"

"Hmm," Zorvut murmured, smiling at Taegan's playful tone. "I do like that white tunic you have with the embroidered gold leaves."

"An excellent choice," he agreed, and went to pull it out of his closet.

"And for me?" Zorvut asked, turning toward his own wardrobe. Taegan frowned in thought, looking him up and down.

"I've always been fond of that burgundy shirt, the first one the tailor made for you," he said, and with a nod Zorvut retrieved it.

They stood at the foot of the bed, each holding their respective shirts in a hesitant silence.

"I love you," Taegan said finally, looking down at the shirt in his hand. "I'm so glad you're home."

There was a soft noise of shifting fabric as Zorvut stepped closer to him, closing the distance between them.

"Thank you for bringing me home," he replied, barely above a whisper, and kissed him gently.

When they had washed away the dust and grime of the road, and changed into their clean clothing, Taegan led the way out to the temple courtyard. Though familiar, it was a quiet contrast to their first meeting;

there were no magical lights floating in the treetops, no decorations set out upon the walkways, no guests watching beyond the curtain of the willow tree as they approached. It was only the two of them, the king in his everyday finery, and the high priest in a plain set of robes, with the temple lit by flickering candles and lanterns in the cool evening air.

But they still stood in front of the elder tree the same way they had the first time, and the priest, Estalar, began his ceremonial words in the same bored tone.

"Prince Taegan, Prince Zorvut. We gather here beneath our elder tree, before each other and the gods, to join these two," he began, sounding exactly as disinterested as he had the last time, and Taegan could not stop himself from smiling in amusement. Zorvut's eyes were locked on his own, and he returned the smile fondly. "Since time immemorial, elves have gathered beneath this tree to bind themselves to each other in marriage. The gods have smiled down on us, that any elf may marry another as an equal and continue our lineage. In exchange for pledging ourselves to one another, the gods give us what is perhaps our greatest gift—our mental bond, formed through ancient magic, so that we are bound not only in word and in heart, but also in mind."

The priest looked between the two of them, for the first time seeming rather uncertain how to proceed, then gestured toward Taegan. "Prince Taegan, if you would give your vows to Prince Zorvut."

"Zorvut," Taegan started, only to find himself suddenly overwhelmed with emotion. He struggled against tears as he spoke. "My love. I pledge myself to you again this day. I vow to love you and support you, to fight alongside you. I vow to guide you and to learn from you. I promise you, we will restore the peace we once had. You have my heart, now and forever. This, I vow to you before the gods and our people."

"Do you find these vows sufficient, Zorvut?"

Tenderly, Zorvut reached out and touched his arm in a comforting motion, his expression soft. "Yes," he replied quietly.

"And Prince Zorvut, if you would give your vows to Prince Taegan."

"My Taegan," he said, his voice a low rumble. "You have proven that there is nothing you would not do for me, and today I pledge the same to you. I vow to protect you, to keep you safe, no matter what happens. I vow to work with you and your people, our people, to restore peace, so we can live out our days together in comfort and happiness. I am yours, as you are mine. This, I vow to you before the gods and our people."

"Do you find these vows sufficient, Taegan?"

Taegan could not stop the silent tears dripping down his face now, and he nodded. "Yes," he said, his voice nearly breaking with emotion.

"Well, you've already joined hands," Estalar said, and he reached over to place his hands over theirs. "Let us re-bind you."

The familiar heat of magic flowed from the priest's fingers onto Taegan's skin, coursing up his arm and into his chest before dispersing through the rest of his body and settling in the familiar pinprick of warmth in the back of his head. There was a moment of overwhelming heat that made him wince, then it faded—and he gasped in the sheer relief of Zorvut's presence in his head again, as if he had been dying of thirst and finally could drink deeply of an endless supply of cold, sweet water. Zorvut's hand squeezed his, and when he looked, he could see that his eyes had slipped closed. But through the bond, he could feel the same relief and joy that echoed his own.

"It is done," the priest said, withdrawing his hands, and Taegan could not hold back a laugh of joy. "Again the gods have smiled upon your union. My princes, I pray your continued bond will restore us to the peace we so briefly enjoyed."

"Thank you," Taegan said breathlessly, nodding. Behind him, he could hear King Ruven shift, lifting a hand to wipe at his eyes.

"Yes, thank you," the king repeated as the priest stepped down from the raised platform, and they walked together toward the entrance of the temple, leaving the two princes alone before the elder tree.

"My love," Zorvut murmured, and pulled Taegan close to his chest. In his familiar embrace, the rest of the world faded away. If they were together, they could do anything, peace treaty or not. He had never been more sure of anything in his life.

TO BE CONTINUED

# About the Author

Lionel Hart (he/him) is an indie author of MM fantasy romance and paranormal romance. Currently, he resides in north San Diego with his husband and their dog. For personal updates and new releases, follow the links below.

Twitter: @lionelhart_

Facebook: Lionel Hart, Author

TikTok: @author.lionelhart

Email Newsletter

# Also By Lionel Hart

### **Chronicles of the Veil**
1. The Changeling Prophecy
2. The Drawn Arrow
3. Coming 2022

### **The Orc Prince Trilogy**
1. Claimed by the Orc Prince
2. Blood of the Orc Prince
3. Ascension of the Orc King

### **Heart of Dragons Duology**
1. Beneath His Wings
2. Coming 2022

Printed in Great Britain
by Amazon